I0666926

# The Man In The Sodden Cap

S.W. Campbell

Published by Shawn Campbell

The Man In The Sodden Cap

ISBN: 979-8-9870287-0-4

To Aunt Alma, the woman who lived her life her way, taught me to love and respect the land, and showed everyday that anything can be overcome with a little care and common sense.

*The Man In The Sodden Cap*

# Table of Contents

# Preface

In the fall of 2013, my mother pointedly asked me why I wrote so few happy or funny stories. It was a fair question. Looking back over the early years of my writing, while not all of my writing was dramatic or depressing, a vast majority of what I wrote could by no means be considered lighthearted. Over the years I've had multiple therapists and other psychological types tell me that writing is an excellent way of lightening one's mental burdens and judging by what I wrote in those early years, I must have had a lot of unburdening to do.

Though I had written a little before, this focused unburdening really began to gain steam in 2013. In that single year I wrote over 50 short stories, nearly half of which were written in the three months of spring. Many of these stories can be found in this collection, with others in the short story collections *An Unsated Thirst* and *Stumptown*. The sheer volume of stories written over a relatively short period of time seems crazy today, but apparently once the dam was broken, there was no way to reseal the breach. Thoughts, worries, memories, and more all came pouring out in a mass of fiction, biography, and strange mixtures between the two. The only thing that seems crazier is that the number would have been even higher, but for the fact that I began writing my first novel, *The Uncanny Valley*, in the summer of that year, giving myself a viable alternative to the seemingly unending vomiting of my soul via my short stories.

It's a strange thing to go back and look through these short stories. Many of them make me cringe somewhat, some include a quality of writing that is somewhat subpar, but some of them to this day remain some of my most favorite stories that I've ever written. These were some of the first stories that I really wanted to share with the world, partly because I had the desperate need of a man just turning thirty for the world to understand, but also because I wanted to let people with similar experiences know that they were not alone, and that things were going to be all right, even though I wasn't entirely sure of such a premise myself.

The year 2013 was the first year that I began actively sending out short stories to be published, a painful affair which resulted in nothing but 70 rejections. With the hindsight of some 3,700 rejections today, this seems like a laughably low number, but at the time it was a devastating blow only slightly softened by the occasional kind words of encouragement included in what was otherwise a seemingly unending march of form letters. Your first time is always the hardest, because for the first time you're fully opening yourself up to the world. My first short story publication wouldn't come until the following year, "The Heartbreaker", which is the second story in this collection.

In many ways I miss those early days of writing. There was a lot of hope involved in it. It was a nice combination of hope that somehow this would all lead to amazingly big things meshed with the sense that if nothing happened so what, only voluntary time had been invested and it was a fun distraction.

Things didn't have to be poignant, but it was infused beautifully with the belief that everything could be. It was okay to share anything I felt like I needed to say, because realistically the chances of anyone reading it was pretty damn slim. In other words, it was a beautiful mess of contradictions.

I can't really imagine going back to writing at such a pace again, though it was a pace I managed to continue through 2019, with the exception of 2015 for whatever reason. I think it's less that I'm no longer able to sustain such a pace, just that as the world has changed, I have found myself with a greater number of more pressing real world distractions. Perhaps when the world slows down I can return to such output again, if my interests have not changed by then.

It's strange to compare the stories in this collection to the earlier stories contained in *An Unsated Thirst*. In many ways, the stories in this collection are much for inward facing. Though some of my earlier writing tried to explore the wider world beyond myself, throughout 2013 the central theme seemed fully locked on to my own experiences, something that would not begin to change until the world started moving into 2014. I'm not sure what to make of this little factoid, but I imagine writing is much like most things in life, wherein it is much easier to be empathetic when our own houses are in order, something that cannot be accomplished without a bit of navel gazing.

Anyways, I'm beginning to ramble a bit here, and you of course aren't here to read the preface, but rather the stories which follow. This short story collection, which for whatever reason I've opted to entitle *The Man in the Sodden Cap*, contains twenty-six short stories written between March and November of 2013, a period of literary angst, with a couple of humorous episodes and inklings of focusing onto the broader world thrown in for good measure. I hope you enjoy reading them, and that in reading them you find parts of yourself in this shared mess we call humanity.

Before I close, I would just like to add one thing. Given the nature of these stories, many contain references to people both living and dead, both directly, and via less than clever name changes. For anyone who catches sight of themselves or someone they know in these stories, I hope you know they represent just a point in time of both of our lives. Short stories specifically rarely capture the full breadth of a person. They are but a sliver of a moment, with viewpoints, emotions, and actions frozen by the limited confines of the words on the page. They are all incomplete stories. Happy reading.

# One Night In Rapid City

It's your everyday hotel room. Two queen beds with plain tan comforters. A chair in the corner under a lamp, its cover matching the drapes on either side of the tall window that looks down six stories to the parking lot. A large flat screen television on top of an unused dresser, the time of occupancy not long enough to warrant taking the clothes out of the bag on the floor. A desk against the wall with a simple plastic and vinyl desk chair that can be purchased in bulk from any office supply company. A tiny bathroom through a door near the entrance. Bad low cost artwork hangs on the walls. Geometric shapes in inoffensive shades of brown. The door to the outside world is bolted. The chance of a stray murderer coming into the hotel and picking that one random door out of the hundreds just like it apparently too high to risk not locking it.

He sits at the desk in front of his laptop, looking aimlessly at websites to try and entertain himself as much as possible. The television blares with some shitty movie on HBO. It doesn't matter what's on. He watches HBO because he doesn't have it at home. The curtains are open, allowing a view of the large windowless concrete block that's the building across the street. Just one more distraction to help pass the time. All of the work for the day has been done. The meetings have been attended. Emails have been answered. There is nothing left to do. He's just wasting time now, waiting for something to happen. He knows nothing is going to happen.

Through the locked door is a balcony. Below is the lobby, restaurant, and bar. He can hear the sounds of his fellow conference goers and other mixed guests. Drinking and chatting. A constant murmur in the background, occasionally punctuated by a sharp burst of laughter which cuts across the air. Nice people, assholes, strangers, and colleagues. None of them can really be called friends.

His head is a little cloudy. His belly is full of various hors d'oeuvres, puff pastries, and shrimp. How many shrimp should one really eat when this far from the ocean? Apparently quite a few. How many beers did he drink? Was it four, five, or six? Six seems like a low number. Back in college six was the number of beers he drank before heading out for the night. Just a warm up exercise. He doesn't drink that much beer now. It's probably a good thing. Whatever the exact number, it was exactly one less than what it would take to get truly drunk. He's reached an age where professional and personal require two separate lives.

The entire day has been spent making small talk and politely laughing at bad jokes with people he barely knows. He needs a rest. He needs to be alone. He doesn't mind social interactions. He even enjoys them. He just needs to be alone now and again. He needs to be by himself. Alone with his own thoughts. It's the only way to recharge his batteries. It's always been that way, for as long as he can remember.

The movie plays on. Some aliens in a department store. A band of misfits saves the day. The ending is just as bad as the rest. Who green lights this shit? He sits in the desk chair, butt ass naked. His ass cheeks make little indents in the cushion. His bare skin sticks to the vinyl. He's naked because he's often naked. He enjoys the feeling of sitting around without clothes on. He doesn't tell people about it. It's just something he does. The curtains are open. No one can see him. The hotel is the tallest building around.

In his head he makes up a little story. A story where he's naked in a hotel room because he doesn't have a chance to do such things at home. That's the appeal. Similar to the HBO, it's another silver lining of staying in a hotel in a city surrounded by strangers. You can do whatever you want as long as you're behind the safety of the locked door. He can't be naked at home. He has responsibilities. It would be inappropriate for a grown man to gallivant around his house naked in front of his wife and kids.

None of this is true. He gallivants around his house naked all the time. Gallivant, that's a funny word, you don't hear it that often, but here it is just randomly popping into his head. A little linguistic surprise. He'll probably use it in a conversation sometime tomorrow. Once a word gets into his head it's hard to get it out. He doesn't have a wife or kids. The whole naked thing a may be a little weird, but it's okay from a legal aspect.

It's a nice story. It's a nice thought. It feels good to imagine the other person in his head whose life took a different direction. The man he thought he would be at thirty back when he was twenty, then twenty-five, then twenty-seven, then twenty-eight. The man in his head may not be as successful in his job. The man may not have travelled as much, or seen so much of the world. He really doesn't know much about the man. He's never given the man in his head a full back story beyond having a family.

He thinks about getting up and getting a snack from the vending machine. He ate dinner already, but he's still hungry. It would be nice to have a little snack, but of course then he would have to leave the room. If he left the room he would have to put on some clothes. In all fairness, he doesn't have to put on clothes. Nobody has to do anything, but given the high likelihood of losing his job if he doesn't put on clothes, he pretty much has to. He'd have to leave the room and look down over the balcony at the tiny people talking below. He'd have to walk clear around the circle of the balcony. He'd have to ride the elevator down to the fifth floor. He'd have to walk back around the circle of the balcony to the other side where the vending machines are. Then he'd have to repeat the journey in reverse to get back to his sanctuary.

It would be a long time to be outside the room. It would be a long time to be vulnerable. With his luck there would probably be someone outside their room on the balcony, or someone riding the elevator, or someone at the vending machine. He'd have to make small talk that he doesn't really want to make. At the very least he'd have to make eye contact and acknowledge another person's existence. He doesn't feel like faking it anymore today. He's not neurotic about these things. It's not fear or anxiety that makes him feel as he does. These feelings aren't a constant in his life, but he feels them right now. This is his me time and he doesn't want anyone to interrupt it. He needs it as much as he needs to breathe, or eat, or shit.

The grumble of his stomach makes a more convincing argument. He grabs a pair of shorts from the open suitcase on the floor and slips them on. He puts on a shirt, still damp with sweat from his run that afternoon. He walks over to the door. His hand is on the handle. He takes a deep breath, then another. The murmur outside is louder closer to the door. He begins to press down on the door handle, but stops. He remembers the jerky in the gift bag that everyone was given at the beginning of the conference. He remembers thinking how stupid it was to have jerky in a gift bag. It's still stupid, but he's glad that it's there.

He walks back to the bed and finds the jerky. He takes back off his clothes. He doesn't have to go out. He gets to stay in the womb, warm and safe. The jerky is salty and sweet with the flavor of teriyaki. Boxing comes on the television. He flips through the channels and stops at another shitty movie, this one about halfway through. He sits and chews on the jerky, watching, but not really engaged. He opens another package from the gift bag. This one contains some kind of meat stick made out of buffalo. It tastes terrible. He eats it anyways.

He's rather good at what he does. He's never been one to seek people out. It's always been the other way around. When he's in a big group of people he always feels a little anxious, a little out of place. He can overcome it when he needs to. He can start a conversation and even keep one going for a while. He's good at jokes. Snappy one liners. His mind is quick. He can overcome what some would call shyness, he just doesn't want to. He hates the clothes he has to wear at these meetings. They're always uncomfortable and never feel like they fit right. Maybe that's part of why he always feels so anxious. He hates the polite holding back of the wild thoughts that run through everybody's heads.

A small white piece of quartz sits on the desk next to his laptop. One side is bright white. The other side is gray with dirt. He doesn't actually know if it's quartz, but when he had first looked at it that was the word that had popped into his head. It had just seemed right. He had taken a geology class in college, but he doesn't remember much of it. Mostly just the lisping South African accent of the professor and laughing with his friends when they talked about the schists. The brown schists, the green schists, and the silver schists. They had gone on a field trip where the professor drove the van and talked constantly about his hope of seeing Mount Saint Helens erupt again. The professor wouldn't run yellow lights. It had all seemed pretty funny at the time.

He holds the white rock in his hand. He had picked up the rock earlier that day between the meetings and dinner. He had changed out of his uncomfortable slacks and button down shirt and gone for a run. Streets gave way to a park, which gave way to a golf course, which gave way to tall hills criss crossed by mountain bike paths. It was a warm day. He had taken his shirt off and ran all the way to the top. He had stood and looked down one side at the city and down the other at the Black Hills. His knee hadn't hurt too much. It would probably hurt tomorrow morning. It had been a good run. Elation, happiness without reason. Smiling at the feeling of just being alive. All just a rush of endorphins. A potent drug. Emotions are just chemicals in the brain, but that doesn't mean they're a bad thing. He had picked up the rock without really knowing why. It had been just sitting on the ground. A single piece of quartz all by itself on top of a hill of sandstone.

He takes the rock into the bathroom and washes the dirt off of it. The gray falls away revealing the white underneath. Some of the dark grit doesn't fall away. He rubs at it with a washcloth for a bit, but to no avail. The dirt will just have to stay where it is for now. He walks back to the desk and sits back down. For a moment he thinks about her. It's been awhile since he has thought of her. In the middle of a meeting today she had crossed his mind. It had been a boring meeting. His mind had wandered.

A word had been said, a memory had been triggered, and his eyes had started to water. All of the yearning for the lost joy, all the hurt from the slow and painful death of the relationship, all of the sacrifice, all of the mistakes. It had all come back. A punch to his chest. It has been a long time since the memories have evoked such a strong reaction. Usually they come and go without much fuss. A scar from the past, no longer an issue of the present. A ghost in the silence. A momentary sadness and then the mind moves on.

The second shitty movie comes to an end. He turns off the laptop and gets up. Teeth are brushed. Contacts are taken out. Lights are turned off. It's time for bed. The story restarts in his head. The family man calls his wife and kids to tell them all goodnight. The man's nightly ritual when he's away on business trips. Does the family man have two kids or one? Are they boys or girls? He doesn't know. That part shifts with every telling. The family man's life is blurry and inconsistent. Part of him yearns for the life of the family man in his head. Another part doubts that he really wants the responsibility, that he really wants to give up his freedom for that kind of commitment. The imaginary man in his head is just the grass on the other side of the fence. Not necessarily better, but something different. A person whom it's all right to feel jealous of because it's just himself in an alternative reality.

It's been a long time since he's been in love. It's been a long time since he has come across someone and thought to himself, this one, this is the one. He meets people, he attracts people, but nothing really ever seems to stick. With many he just can't seem to get himself to really give a damn about them. It's like being numb. Some of them he's truly fond of. These are the ones where he can pretend for a little while that he has the feeling again, but in the end he has to stop pretending, and it comes time to move on. He has a good life. He has good friends. He has several nieces and nephews who universally think of him as their favorite uncle. He has so much more than he used to. So much more than he ever did when she was in his life. Perhaps it will all be enough.

He lays in the bed and watches a late night show on television. He considers masturbating but decides not to. He's pretty tired. Maybe in the morning. The rush of endorphins is always a nice way to start the day. Soon he will be going home. One and a half more days of meetings. His thoughts wander to the woman he was with the night before he left. His mind's eye brushes across her curves. His hands caress skin that isn't there. A few too many drinks, some harmless flirting, then back to her place. She lived in a cramped apartment above an Ethiopian restaurant. The bedroom didn't have a door and throughout her little dog would run in and jump on the bed before being shooed out. Maybe he would call her when he got back. He had said he would. Maybe not.

He turns off the television and pulls up the comforter. He closes his eyes. Tomorrow he will be social. Tomorrow he will hang out with people more. Spend more time making small talk and telling bad jokes. It will be enjoyable. Tomorrow they're supposed to go to Mount Rushmore in the evening. That will be fun. He's never been to Mount Rushmore before. He's brought his camera so he can take the same picture that thousands of tourists have taken before him. He will look at the picture and feel like a photographer of great talent, then forget he ever took it. Soon he will be going home. He wants to be home right now. When he gets home he will want to be somewhere else. Not a different place, he likes where he lives, just a different reality. This reality isn't so bad. He smiles and drifts off to sleep. It's been a nice little vacation from the world. It's been nice to be alone.

# The Heartbreaker

I'm sitting in my chair, reading and watching the rain fall against the window. It's a light rain. A soft rain combined with the unusual warmth of early spring throwing arcing rainbows across the sky. It's the best kind of rain. It's midday. My phone rings. I pick it up and look at the caller ID. There's no name, just a number. Somebody I don't know. It's an Idaho number. I went to college in Idaho. My curiosity is peaked. I hit the button to connect.

"Hello."

The voice on the other end is nervous sounding, male. The voice sounds surprised to hear mine.

"Hello? Katie?"

"No, this is not Katie."

"Is Katie there?"

"No. There's no Katie here."

"Are....are you sure?"

"Yes. I've had this number for close to seven years. I'm pretty sure."

I can hear everything in his silence. I can hear the gears grinding in his head. I can hear the moment when realization floods across his brain. The sudden release of breath. The sudden change of nervous hope to disappointment and defeat.

"Oh."

The other end hangs up. I go back to my reading.

I'm driving to the hash. It's a beautiful Saturday. The sun is shining and wind from my open window blows across my left arm laying on the door. It's going to be a good day. I'm looking forward to the run. My phone rings. It's an unknown number from Idaho.

"Hello."

"Hey Katie, it's Matt."

This one is cocky sounding, like he owns the fucking world. I can picture him in my mind. Polo shirt with a popped collar. Baseball cap with a flat brim turned backwards on his head. Probably two fake diamond studs in his ears. More parody than person. This is probably unfair. College aged douchebags have probably changed how they dress since I completed my studies.

"Who?"

"Matt. We met at the Corner Club last night."

I recognize the name of the bar. It's one of the more popular hangouts for students at the University of Idaho. A squat pile of smoke filled cinder blocks selling thirty-two ounce tubs of beer for $2.25. Come to the club for a tub. Good memories.

"This isn't Katie's number."

"What?"

I hear a bit of the cocky edge recede from his voice. It makes me feel happy. There's something in the guy's tone that makes me glad he's getting knocked down a notch.

"This isn't Katie's number."

"This is the number she gave me."

"Don't know what to tell you."

I can hear him breathing on the other end, trying to figure out his next move. Trying to come to grips with the fact that a woman was just trying to get rid of him, the most amazing man in the world. I hang up the phone.

I'm making myself dinner at home. I'm having a T-bone steak and some mashed potatoes. The smell of cooking meat wafts through my apartment. My mouth waters in anticipation. The phone rings. It's an unknown Washington number.

"Hello."

"Hello?"

The voice on the other end sounds confused. It's a tone I'm starting to get used to hearing.

"Hello."

"Is this Katie?"

It's been a slow day. I'm bored. I affect a falsetto voice that would fool no one.

"Yes, yes this is Katie."

"Katie? Really?"

"No dumb ass, you've been given a false number."

The other side of the line disconnects. I hang up and put down my phone. I wish I hadn't done the voice. It had to have been bad enough discovering that some girl lied to your face just to get rid of you. Getting fucked with by some asshole can't be any help. I can see the poor schmuck in my head. I can see him overcoming his nervousness enough to talk to a girl. I can see him filled with pride and boasting to his friends about his acquisition of her digits. I can see him sitting on his couch holding his phone, nerving himself up to actually calling. I can see the uncertainty when he hears my voice. I can see the disappointment when the truth dawns on him. It all has to be bad enough without me being a jackass.

My phone rings. Yet another unknown number. I know what this call will entail even before I answer. It's become a common occurrence. Nearly every weekend. Katie has been out on the town again. I know nothing about this woman, yet I have somehow become part of her life, connected by a string of jilted men she has no interest in ever seeing again. It's starting to get old. I wish Katie would spend more weekends staying home and studying.

"Hello."

The voice is nervous and confused. Just like all the others.

"Hello, is Katie there?"

"No, no Katie here. You have the wrong number."

The phone goes dead. Less than a minute later it rings again.

"Hello."

It's the same confused nervous voice, now tinged by realization and disappointment.

"This isn't Katie's number, is it?"

"No, sorry man."

The phone goes dead. I put my phone down and stare at the wall in front of me. I feel bad for this one. It seems weird that this one bothers me. He's just another distant voice in a long line of anonymous faces. Just another person I'll never meet or know except for thirty seconds of their spirit getting dashed and their confidence crushed. In my head he's just a normal guy. Not a bad guy. Certainly not the best looking or most charming, but still a guy with a lot to offer. In my head he's me.

How many has it been now? Somewhere around at least fifteen. There's been nervous ones and confident ones.

There's been douchey ones and drunk ones. There's even been a foreign one or two. No matter how they start, they all end the same way. Could they all be worth so little? Are none of them even worth a little honesty? What did all these poor schmucks do to deserve having their emotions fucked with? It's one thing to crash while you're still on the ground. It's another to do it when you're flying high above the clouds. I feel like I'm the one who rejected the poor sap. I've done nothing, yet I feel like a jerk.

The phone rings. I hurriedly wipe my ass and pull my pants up. I've been expecting an important call. I've been playing phone tag all day. I can't let this one get by. I'm not done wiping. I'm not even done with the precursor to wiping. It doesn't matter. My pants go up and I waddle to my phone on the table in the kitchen. One more ring and it goes to voicemail. I open it just in time.

"Hello."

My voice sounds strained. The voice of a man who just beat his personal best in a triathlon.

"Hello. Is Katie there?"

I feel the muscles in my neck tighten. I feel the veins in my head begin to bulge. This has gone too far. This is too fucking ridiculous. How many fake numbers can one woman hand out? What is it about her that causes every jerk in town to line up and wait their turn to have their wings clipped? What kind of magic spell does she weave? Why must I be a part of her assembly line of shattered hopes and broken hearts? Something in me snaps. I can't take it anymore. My voice booms with thunder, full of wrath brought down from the heavens themselves.

"No, Katie is not here. Katie has never been here. This isn't Katie's number. Katie gave you a fake number because she just wanted to get rid of you. I'm sorry. It sucks. If you do see her cunt ass again would you mind telling her to get the fucking balls to reject somebody to their face, or at the very least, use someone else's phone number."

The phone goes dead on the other end. I waddle back to the bathroom.

# Chariots In The Sky

The journey has been several hours to the outskirts of Pasco. The green rolling waves of the Palouse have given way to emptiness. Acres of bare hills, basalt outcroppings, and sagebrush punctuated by the occasional verdant splash of irrigated fields. Potatoes, onions, alfalfa. Little patches of oasis in the wasteland which the freeway passes through. It has been some time since John has driven this route. Some time since he has made this journey. But the landmarks are all familiar and the same.

Random buildings and structures dot the landscape. Houses, barns, potato sheds, phone towers, tractors, and the occasional freeway exit onto empty and unexplored roads. A long line of monstrous metal men, skeletons of girders, march across the landscape holding up high voltage power lines, carrying the miracle of electricity from the hydroelectric dams in the wastes to the major population centers of the West Coast. Trucks and cars speed along with him. John passes some and they fall behind. Others pass him and disappear into the distance. None match the velocity at which he speeds. All move forward or fall back. Time moves faster or slower depending upon the object's relative position to his own. It has been a long drive. A long week. John is growing tired.

Great white clouds hang in the sky overhead. Hundreds of individual balls of puff that stretch from horizon to horizon. A great aeronautical border surrounding a patch of blue sky above. They hang like two great flotillas facing off across the heavens. Battleships, cruisers, destroyers, frigates, and corvettes. Waiting to unleash destruction upon each other and those unfortunate enough to find themselves in between. Both sides are holding until the opening shot. They hang silent and unmoving, waiting for the other side to break the unofficial truce. Electricity fills the air. John can feel the hair on his arms rise with anticipation. Below, the people, ants to the warships in the sky, wait with baited breath for their fates to be decided by the overhanging gods.

Soon John will be in Pasco, and the latest segment of his journey will be done. The car smells ripe with sweat, flatulence, empty snack wrappers, and the little bits of soda always left at the bottom of the cans. John has been living out of the car for the past week. A business trip that has been far too long. This is just a side trip. Business took him close enough, so he took off the extra day to take the extra time. This is the last stop before he heads for home. It has been a good trip. John is alone, but he has not once felt lonely on the long drive. This is a rarity.

John's cousin and his cousin's wife have welcomed into the world a new family member just eleven weeks prior. The baby is barely out of the grub stage, most likely barely even starting to exhibit a personality. That is the purpose of the journey. To see the new life that has been brought forth. To coo and tell his cousin and his cousin's wife that they've done a good job. To count the fingers and toes and judge whether or not the squalling pink bundle makes eye contact long enough and shows enough interest in the surrounding world. It is a good thing. It is a blessing. John likes babies. They hold his attention better than most other things. He is always amazed at the miracles which his friends and family bring forth. It is doubtful that he will ever have his own.

Off in the distance, above the remote hills, the tension between the two great fleets of clouds in the sky breaks. At first it is only a few small flashes. They have been steadily moving closer together, and now forces of hatred and fear can no longer be held back. The few small flashes grow and spread. Laser light, green, red, yellow, and blue, criss cross the divide. Explosions begin to appear on the surfaces of the far off vessels. The battle has been joined. The fate of the galaxy hangs in the balance.

Melanie? Maude? Minerva? John can't remember the new baby's name. This is his cousin's and his cousin's wife's second child. He can't remember the first child's name either. It has been a long time since John has visited his cousin. All three of them had lived in Calgary at the same time. It had never been planned. Things had just kind of happened that way. They had been the anchor in John's life. The island of known in the great sea of unknown. John had moved back so he could see his family more. He saw most of them now about as much as he did before he moved back. He saw his cousin a lot less. This was unfortunate.

The gunners in the distant vessels begin to find their range. The explosions begin to intensify. Smaller vessels become overwhelmed. They cannot handle the concentrated firepower. Burning and breaking up they fall from the sky, hitting the ground below out of view of John's speeding car. Over Pasco the skies remain empty. The fleets on either side do not dare move forward to do battle. They cannot risk fighting over Pasco. They cannot risk damaging or destroying the device. Instead they launch long-range missiles at each other, tracing long contrails across the blue emptiness. A salvo leaps from left to right across the sky. An answering salvo leaps from right to left. Nipping at each other, but not biting.

An old livestock auction barn rushes by the window to the right. Its paint is old and shabby, peeling in the desert sun. The sign nailed to the side of the barn is faded. The fences have seen better days. Only the rows of semis and cattle trailers, pickups and goosenecks, give evidence that the yard is still in operation. A small plane sits in a nearby field. Is it for the auctioneer, so he can quickly move on to another show, or is it owned by some rich cowpoke who comes from some far off place? John does not know, and does not care enough to stop to find out.

One man fighters are launched and begin to dart into the empty spaces between the fleets. Each side vying for aerial dominance in the area forbidden to the larger ships. Sonic booms echo across the heavens as they twist and turn, maneuvering to gain an advantageous position. Laser light leaps forward and explosions ripple across the sky. Below, the ants continue to drive their vehicles forward at reckless speeds, some going towards the city and some away. Nobody is sure which is the safer course of action. It all seems so calm and orderly. If one never looked at the sky they could believe it was just a normal Thursday afternoon.

John looks down at his gauges. He only has a quarter tank of gas left. He will have to remember to fill it up tomorrow morning before he moves on. The car always needs to be filled up. Its gas tank is small, only twelve gallons. The little car is not the most comfortable car in the world, but it gets good gas mileage. The last time he had calculated, it had been at 35.7 miles per gallon. That put the average for the trip so far at 34.5. Not too shabby.

The professor had told him that the two sides had been fighting for generations. All others had been swept aside until it was just the two of them, vying for galactic domination. One side believes in an unseen god, led by prophets, taking into account omens and signs. The other believes in a logical model of the universe, led by engineers, taking into account equations and well tested theories. The device is the only thing that can break the stalemate. An ancient artifact of immense power and unknown origin. The gift of the gods, or beings so advanced they might as well have been gods. Whoever controls the device will control the galaxy. Generations of searching have led them to this galactic backwater. John does not know how the professor knows all this. He just knows that his job is to get the professor to the device.

Irrigation pivots slide by to either side, supplied with water by canals from the distant river. Corn, potatoes, onions, mint, wheat, sugar beets, and alfalfa. Artificial rain creating gardens in a land meant for cheat grass and sagebrush. No one walks in the fields that John drives past. The crops are all still small, only the alfalfa will be harvested soon. The rest are still a month or so off. The farmers are all in their sheds readying their tractors for the upcoming burst of action.

The fields crawl with the troops of the U.S. Army. Some ready anti-aircraft guns while others unload ammunition from trucks. The grunts just mill around, standing next to humvees and tanks, unsure what to do. Their weapons are useless in the battle overhead. Harrier jets take off from hangars disguised as potato sheds. Neither side in the great battle cares about the primitive inhabitants of the world. To them, the people of Earth and their weak defenses, are just a small sideshow to the grand theater of the confrontation above.

The professor has hypothesized that humans are the direct descendants of the guardians of the device. Defenders left by the ancient creators to make sure that it never fell into the wrong hands. If this is true than humans have fallen a long ways down the food chain. Bullets, missiles, and rockets. The best of our weapons are ineffective against the invaders. They are but the biting of gnats. All it gains is the attention of the superior beings. Single pilot attack fighters dive down from the heavens. Harrier jets fall from the sky. Laser light melts men and guns alike. Hangars disguised as potato sheds catch fire. Some soldiers scatter and run. Some continue to blast away, pockets of resistance, shooting at the sky with useless ferocity.

Two children will make it more difficult for John's cousin and John's cousin's wife, but they will be able to handle it. John thinks of them as good parents. He knows they will do an excellent job. He had wondered when they had first got married. He had wondered if his cousin was making the right choice. John had even pulled his cousin aside at the bachelor party to drunkenly ask him if he was sure he was making the right decision. His cousin had been sure of himself. Time had proven his cousin right. John was not too proud to admit when he was wrong. To others or to himself. Looking back, John wonders how he could have ever questioned such a thing. The pair seem natural together. He always looks forward to seeing both of them.

The number of buildings alongside the road begin to grow thicker. More exits begin to branch off of the freeway. John has reached the outskirts of Pasco. Where once there were fields and sagebrush, now there are gas stations and tractor dealerships. Random businesses dot the landscape. John wonders who would drive this far from the center of town to buy a hot tub or a car. It doesn't really matter. Somebody obviously must. Just an idle thought in an idle head. A tall granary, a mass of concrete, sits along the road, stabbing upward into the sky.

The granary explodes, its concrete walls shattering, the golden harvest within spilling out onto the ground. Some of the one man fighters have grown bored of destroying each other and the remnants of the U.S. military. They have begun strafing the random buildings on the outskirts of the city. The professor cowers in the back seat, covering his head with his hands. He is a learned man, an educated man. He is not a brave man. For the professor, problems are on blackboards, not moving overhead spreading death before them. This is why John is here.

John keeps the car moving forward. What else can he do? The car is such a small and fragile thing compared to the grandeur of the battle all around. But it is all that John has. His mission is key. Nothing else matters. The sky is only a distraction. John constantly finds himself staring up into it. Watching the battle and not the traffic. He constantly has to shift his attention back and forth in order to both avoid an accident, And take in the terrible grandeur.

Contact fluid. He forgot to get contact fluid at his last stop. The bottle ran out this morning and if he doesn't get more than he won't be able to take out his contacts tonight. John could sleep with them in. He has done it before, but it's not pleasant. If he does, his eyes will feel dried out for the rest of the next day. Better to make sure he gets contact fluid. There are drug stores and retail stores where he turns off to get to his cousin's house. It has been a few years since John's been in the Tri-Cities, but he doubts they have been torn down since. He should go to a department store, not a drug store. Buy a few little toys. A gift for the new baby, and a gift to keep the new baby's sister from getting jealous.

Overhead, a large cruiser begins to move over the city, three opposing corvettes move forward to block its progress. They fire precisely, aiming to destroy weapons, not bring each other down. This is a risky strategy, moving ships over Pasco and the device. John looks in his rearview mirror. Behind him he sees giant men built of steel girders marching forward on four thin legs. At the end of each hulking giant's down stretched arms, laser cannons unleash their fury at anything that comes too close. In front across the hillsides, above the city, an opposing force appears. Great white towers waving three large arms in the air. To the untrained eye they could almost be mistaken for wind turbines, but John recognizes them as the machines of war they are. Both sides have landed ground troops. The final acts of the campaign are near.

Traffic gets thicker as John moves farther into the city. The hectic forward pace drops from seventy miles per hour, to forty-five, to thirty. The constant forward velocity breaks down into stop and go movements. Distances become measured in car lengths. At first John feels his anxiety spike. His desperation to move on does not match his present reality. His legs shake and his hands clutch the steering wheel, tightening and loosening rhythmically. But the adrenaline flowing through his veins lessens. His body settles into the new reality.

The fireworks overhead suddenly come to a halt, turned off as though by a giant switch. The machines of war, marching across the ground behind and in front, stop moving. One man fighters split off from their dances of death, and return to their respective sides. The world enters an eerie calm. John looks around in shock. One second it was as though everything was collapsing atop him, and now all the debris hangs floating in the air. Something has stopped the madness. Something has happened.

The professor is no longer cowering. He's listening to a shortwave radio with excitement, muttering scientific jargon to himself. As full realization takes place he raises his head and jabbers excitedly at John.

"They can't land. All their ground troops are dying. A nanovirus. Definitely biological, but most likely artificial. It's adapting too fast. They can't stop it. It's only affecting their ground troops." The professor notices John's look of confusion. "Don't you see? We're not the guardians of the device. We are only the hosts of the guardians. It's like those science fiction books. The germs my friend, it's the germs."

The line of vehicles continues to snake its way slowly forward. The shock of the sudden end to the fighting is surprisingly like rush hour traffic. People leaving their jobs and heading home to make dinner and relax in the sunshine. John's eyes trace across damaged buildings and smoke rising in the air, all is ignored by the other drivers. Downtown has not been hit as hard as the outskirts, but it has still been hit. The slow snake of cars and trucks passes over the river on the old familiar blue bridge. John is amazed that it wasn't damaged at all. John, now in Kennewick, steers the car onto the correct exit and drives up a major thoroughfare. The great white towers of the war machines on the hills above stand stationary, only their long arms moving in broad circles.

The light ahead turns red and John stops. Hispanic music pours from the open window of the car next to his. A Mexican pop band playing an upbeat and happy tune. A group of Mexican laborers fill the front and back seats, coming home from their menial jobs for menial pay. Chasing the American dream. They want what everybody wants, to not feel so small, to not feel so powerless and insignificant. The light turns green and together they move forward.

John cannot remember why he was rushing. Why was he so desperate to get where he was going? Soon the trip will be over. Tomorrow he will drive the last leg. Tomorrow he will get home to his empty house and make for himself a solitary dinner. John is happy to visit his cousin and his cousin's family. His cousin's house will be full of people. Full of life. Full of people glad to see him. John's house is not like that. John is happy for his cousin, but a part is also jealous. John is ashamed of the jealousy, but cannot deny that it is there.

The radio is off, but it suddenly blares to life. Across the planet every radio, television, cell phone, and CB channel starts to broadcast. It is a message from the leader of the religious alien fleet. The gods have doomed all who step upon the surface of the holy planet. Therefore the humans must deliver the device to the chosen ones. If they fail to do so then the Earth will be bathed in holy fire until none are left alive.

All goes silent, then sound blares forth once again. This time it is the aliens of science and theorems. The device cannot be trusted to the superstitious and the believers in mystics. The device must be delivered to those who will use it with reason and logic. If mankind fails to deliver the device to them, then they will have no choice but to destroy all life on the planet.

John drives in stunned silence. Around him the world is gripped in such a state of disbelief that it is as if nobody even heard the demands. It is the professor who breaks the silence. They have no choice, they must continue forward and activate the device. John asks him if he knows what will happen if the device is activated. The professor tells him no, but what other choice do they have? Do nothing, the world is destroyed. Give the device to one of the alien factions, the world is destroyed. Activate the device, maybe the world is destroyed, maybe it's not. There are no other options. They have no other choice.

John makes a turn off the main boulevard and then another into a broad parking lot. The large red, white, and blue sign is familiar. It is the perfect hiding spot. Right out in the open. Right where everyone and everything can see it. Nobody would ever suspect that the device is hidden beneath a retail box store in eastern Washington. The government built the store when they found the device. They hoped that by understanding it they could begin a golden age. All they accomplished was attracting outside attention. The professor and John get out of the car and jog towards the door. People mill about and go about their day, unaware of the importance of their discount shopping location.

Together, John and the professor, move to the back of the store. The professor uncovers a hidden key pad and types in a code. The grind of hydraulics is heard and shelves full of yarn move away to reveal a hidden elevator which leads into the depths of the Earth. The elevator door opens and the professor moves inside. John tries to follow, but the professor stops him. John does not need to come. Only the professor has the knowledge necessary to activate the device. John would be able to do nothing to help. He would be risking his life for no reason. John is a brave man and a good man. He should get as far away as possible. John needs to live. There is no use in throwing his life away. The elevator doors close and John turns and walks away.

The contact liquid is near the front of the store in the pharmacy section. John walks past aisles containing pain relievers, first aid kits, shampoo, and makeup. He walks down the wrong aisle, then back up the right one. He finds the right area on the shelves. There is the brand John used to use. The old spray can. There is the brand John uses now, with its special lens holder in every box. The box in hand, John walks back towards the rear of the store and the toy aisles.

John wanders through them looking, the ghost feeling of excitement echoing faintly in his mind. Leftovers from a childhood left behind long ago. Most of the aisles are not for girls or are not age appropriate, but he walks through them anyways, enjoying them and remembering. He looks at the stuffed animals. Picks one up. Presses on its paw so it sings songs and makes noises. How many toys does a child really need? His cousin's children already have so much. There are so many better things he can give besides poorly made toys shipped in from overseas. John walks away. He buys his contact liquid and leaves the store.

John walks calmly to his car, his footsteps slow and easy. In his mind he is running as fast as he can. He unlocks the car door and gets in. He puts the key in the ignition and starts the engine. He puts the car into gear. The car drives out of the parking lot. There is only so much time before the professor activates the device. He slowly turns out onto the street. The car in his mind barrels forward at full speed, putting as much distance between it and the device as possible. Stoplight, stop and go, second stoplight, turn right. Take a left then take a right. The car pulls up in front of a nice light blue house on the street corner. A stained wooden fence hides the backyard from the view of the street. A well maintained lawn surrounds the front.

A great blue column of pulsating energy erupts into the sky in the distance. The air blooms with static electricity and the world fills with the crackling sounds of voltage arcing from contact point to contact point. The device has been activated. Thousands of bolts of blue lightning erupt from the column. They leap forward and each finds one of the thousands of warships and small one man fighters that fill the skies above. Explosions rend the air and the mighty juggernauts of destruction disintegrate, consumed by the power of the device, hulls turning from hardened metal to powder. Engines go dead and the hulk fall from the heavens, crashing downward into the wasted desert below. It is a glorious sight to see. A glorious thing to see the skies ripped asunder and the tools of the mighty brought to nothing in a few seconds. The gods torn from their lofty heights as though by a child.

The blue column of energy dissipates and disappears, as though it never was. Silence fills the void. Silence except for the steady hum of the car's engine. John reaches forward and shuts off the key. He gets out of the car and locks the doors. He walks up the sidewalk, gently curving from the street to the front door. John looks back behind him at the sky, and feels a sense of accomplishment. He turns back towards the door and rings the doorbell.

# Knit Your Own Cat

It's strange how the mind works. I'm standing in line at the bookstore, waiting to make my purchases, several new books all suggested by friends. It's been a good day. I feel relaxed and at ease. Nothing can go wrong. Everything feels all right. The line snakes back and forth, going past bookstore branded knick knacks and cutesy books that people only buy on an impulse when they see them while waiting for their turn at the cash register.

The two girls ahead of me are laughing and pointing at one of the books on the low shelves. I look down and read the title. "Knit Your Own Cat." I don't pick it up, but I can visualize the instructions inside, detailing how to make a cat out of yarn. It is not something that I would normally buy, but yet I can still see myself buying it. I can see myself picking it up and putting it on the counter. I can see myself paying money for it and putting it in my bag. I can see myself taking it to her as she laughs and smiles. It is something she would have enjoyed.

The version in my head is just an alternative reality. Something that does not exist. I walk by the book that I know she would love. I feel all of the weight of all that has happened crash back down onto me. A forgotten burden suddenly returned without warning. Cloudy weather on my once sunny day. It will take time to dig myself back out. My day is ruined. There was no way to see it coming.

# The Golden Room

In 1532, Francisco Pizarro conquered the greatest empire in the Americas with only 168 men. The Incan Empire stretched from modern day Colombia to Chile, encompassing an estimated 775,000 square miles and ruling over 20 million people. The Incas were warriors and conquerors. They created their empire from scratch in less than a hundred years. To the other indigenous peoples of the region, they seemed unstoppable. A force of nature. An unbreakable juggernaut.

Pizarro marched into their midst with a motley collection of adventurers numbering a little over half the number of Spartans who died at Thermopylae. Facing an Incan army of 80,000 battle hardened troops, Pizarro, called for a parlay and took their Emperor Atahualpa hostage. To gain his release, Atahualpa filled a room with gold as his ransom. The Spaniards took the gold, and then executed their prisoner. The Inca Empire crumbled into dust, and its people were scattered by civil war and plague. Even in the city that he founded, Lima, Pizarro is cursed as a barbaric butcher. However, whatever one might think of Pizarro, one has to admit that he had balls.

It's strange the things that pop into one's brain when they are doing mindless work. The random thoughts that can float free when efforts become a force of automation, not intellect. The paint roller goes up and down, up and down, up and down. Each upward push resulting in a squishing sound of the paint being forced out of the rolling brush. With each movement, the primer white of the walls and ceiling is replaced by something that the cans call summer splendor. The first coat is nearly three quarters of the way done. The color is not summer splendor. It is too dark. The painted walls and ceiling resemble an inversed bar of gold.

The boss comes in and looks at the work. He watches as the worker refills the paint roller and starts on another section. The boss moves his large frame with surprising ease. His quick and clever eyes survey what has been done so far from beneath an old trucker cap which hides his bald head from the world. One large hand rests on a rotund belly, the other plays with a toothpick which he has taken from his mouth. The worker does not stop. The worker does not look up. Many people have come in to see the new section of the office, the part that when finished, will be a combination conference and break room. He does not want to be bothered. He does not want to break his rhythm.

The boss is a man with balls too. A man who made a lot from a little by taking opportunities when he saw them. When he was a young man he owned nothing. Now he owns one of the larger farms in the area, a fertilizer distribution business, and a 20,000 head feedlot. He is an important man. It is an impressive feat, for someone to go from being a nobody to prominence. It takes intelligence, it takes luck, it takes guts.

Some people would grow large enough and call that good enough. Not the boss. The boss could live a life of leisure, but he can't. The drive to succeed has never left him. It is the sole and complete purpose of his life. To grow, to become stronger, to become bigger. You could give some people the world, and it would not be enough. They would reach for the stars. Rest and relaxation are a foreign thing to the boss. A day off is just a missed opportunity. One day he will stop striving and reaching out for more. On that day he will be dead.

"You wouldn't believe what happened to me driving up from Lethbridge this morning."

"Hmmm." The worker does not stop working. The boss is a person who likes to talk.

"I was driving that new car, you know the one I got from the States, and I was really putting the hammer down. Seeing what she could do. I was probably doing close to 150 k per hour."

The boss has always been a fast driver. Driving is wasted time. Wasted time when one could be watching the markets and looking for new opportunities to grow one's pile of Robert Bordens. It is scary as hell to ride with the boss. Like riding with an overly primed teenager. When the worker has to do it he usually closes his eyes and prays for survival.

"I was a little outside of Vulcan when the RCMP pulled me over. The officer walked up and asked me if I knew how fast I was going. So I say no and he tells me, and I make a big show of being surprised. Then I look down at the speedometer and act all shocked, like I've just realized that the car has an American speedometer and that I thought it was telling me I was going 90 k per hour. The officer looks and sees that I'm right and lets me go with just a warning." The boss begins to laugh. "How dumb do you have to be to think somebody wouldn't notice they were going that fast?"

The worker smiles politely, but continues with his work. The boss eyes the walls with an air of expertise, like an art critic at the Louvre.

"This paint is too dark."

"Yes, it's a little darker than I thought it would be."

"How many gallons of paint do you have?"

"You told me to get it all, so about fifteen gallons or so. I'm not sure how much I have left."

"That's a lot of money."

"Yeah."

"I don't like how dark it is."

"It doesn't look too bad. It will look better when the entire room is finished."

"You should mix some of the primer into the paint that you have, lighten it up a bit."

"I don't really think that's a good idea."

"Why not?"

"I'd probably fuck it up. I wouldn't get it the same from one can to the next."

This is a lie. The worker is completely capable of mixing paint. It's not a hard thing to do. The boss had let the staff choose the color to paint the walls. The staff had chosen summer splendor. What right did he have to demand a change now? Every right, they were his walls, but the worker doesn't care. It is strange the places people decide to draw the line. It is strange the points at which one decides to defy authority.

"It's not that hard. Just get a measuring cup and pour the same amount of primer into each can."

"I'm not comfortable doing it. It wouldn't look good. I could get some different paint if you'd like."

"What the hell would we do with this paint then?"

"I don't know."

The boss is about to say something else when the phone rings in his office. He turns and goes to answer it. The battle is over for now. The worker watches him stalk off and continues painting, turning the walls to gold. It has been building. The storm has been brewing for several months. Little acts of defiance here and there. Little pokes, nothing in themselves, but slowly adding up to a something larger. The storm is soon to break.

It doesn't matter. The worker doesn't have much more time here. Just another month and he'll leave the prairies for a new job in Oregon. It's just a matter of survival now. Just a matter of holding out until it's time to go. He would go now if he could. If it wasn't for a little known tax regulation cooked up by some pencil pushing bureaucrat to fight bastards looking for loopholes. The worker is not a bastard, at least he doesn't think so. He just lives in a world that is full of them. Bastards that just want to get ahead, bastards that make the world more difficult for everybody else.

The painting is soothing. A job where one can look back at the end of day and see all that they have accomplished. It is a good feeling. A feeling from a past life. A life with calloused hands and aching joints. A life of sweaty brows and numb fingers. It was a good life. The job of painting is beneath the worker, a waste of talent. The worker has a master's in economics and commands a salary of seventy thousand per year before taxes. Intellect is expensive. Sweat is cheap. The past few months have been a waste. Before painting the room the worker had been out in the feedyard, picking up old baling twine and other garbage. The worker doesn't mind. He gets paid the same and it is all just a matter of time.

The boss gets off the phone and the worker tenses, expecting him to come back to argue more about the paint, but he doesn't. The office door opens and closes. The engine of a pickup grinds to life and drives away. The worker breaths a little easier. The boss has never been bad to the worker. In fact, he has been quite generous. The worker gets paid a more than fair wage. An impressive wage for somebody who has just gotten out of college. The boss has put a lot of faith in the worker, put a lot of trust into him. The boss has done a lot to help the worker grow and develop. The boss has let the worker explore and pursue ideas. The boss listens to his ideas, even the bad ones.

The boss has been good to his family. Each of the boss's children are employed and are well cared for. Each know that in all likelihood their futures are secure. The boss has been a good provider. The boss loves his family. One of the few things that the boss will stop working for is his family. When his grandkids come into the office they get his entire attention. You can tell that family is important to the boss.

The worker continues his painting. How can you tell someone who has never done anything to you that you have no respect for them? How can you look somebody in the eye who has been nothing but generous and tell them they are greedy? The worker can remember the boss's son coming into his office three months ago; a miniature, thinner, version of the boss. He can remember him looking to make sure nobody else was around to hear.

"Just so you know, we wanted to let you know that we've cut the pay of everyone who works out in the yard. This doesn't affect anybody here in the office, but with all the people coming down from the oil sands it seemed like the smartest thing to do economically."

The recession has hit the oil sands in northern Alberta hard. The drop in the price of oil has made many projects no longer economically viable. Layoffs are widespread and people in their early twenties who had been making six figures have suddenly found themselves without work. The fools, the fools had the world by the tail, and they let it slip through their fingers. Doulee pickups, RV's, ATV's, and speed boats. Wasting it all with the foolish certainty that the sunny days would never end.

All the people coming back south looking for employment made it easy to find people to work in the feedlot. It is not a highly skilled job. It is not that hard to train somebody. It doesn't take long to make somebody proficient enough to get the work done. Economically speaking it is what happens when the labor supply grows. Wages come down. It is nobody's fault. It is just the way the world works. However, it is another thing all together to line up your lowest paid employees and tell them you are going to cut their pay just because you can. It is another thing to look them in the eye and lecture on the invisible hand of Adam Smith as they try to calculate in their heads what parts of their lives they can cut out to make up for the shortfall.

There was no need to do it. The worker has seen the books. He has analyzed the numbers. The feedlot, the farm, the fertilizer plant, they are all doing all right. The recession has certainly caused some harm, but it has not driven things out of the black. It has done nothing but slow the rate of expansion. It was not a situation of I have to do this. It was a situation of I can do this. It's one thing to hire new people at a lower wage. It is another to take the employees who have stayed with you and screw them over. It was a terrible thing to do. A greedy thing to do. A few months later they broke ground on the new conference room. It had been like a slap in the face. How can one look at themselves in the mirror, knowing what has been done?

The day keeps moving forward and the sun moves towards the unseen mountains to the west, just out of sight until the perfect circle is broken by their jagged unseen peaks. The worker puts down the roller and pours the extra paint back into the can. He walks out of the room, now colored gold with its first coat of paint, and turns off the light. He looks back and his heart swells with pride. A good day's work.

# The Rusty Bike

The boys waited until their father put on his warm clothes and went out to feed the animals. The remains of Christmas morning were scattered across the living room. Half assembled plastic toys and games, ripped from the packaging that had once contained them for their shipment across the oceans. Wrapping paper in great piles that swayed with the wind of passing bodies. Santa shaped chocolates and candy canes piled near abandoned stockings. A few empty wrappers gave proof to a first course of breakfast only allowable on holidays. The leavings of another Christmas season coming to an end. All lay forgotten.

The three boys quivered with anticipation as they watched their father walk up the driveway to feed the horses. As soon as he was out of sight they rushed out the backdoor into the garage. Stacks of strategically placed cardboard and other such odds and ends were swiftly moved aside, revealing a buried treasure beneath. The boys looked at it reverently, smiling to themselves with barely contained excitement. There was a short scuffle of words and pushing to decide who got the honor of moving the treasure. In the end, the eldest laid claim since was able to lift it over the step into the house with the greatest ease. They placed the treasure next to the Christmas tree, clearing away the flotsam and jetsam to make room. Together they stood, looking at it, beaming.

It was an old bike. By the shape and style of the frame one would have to assume of an early 1960's vintage. The boys had discovered it one day while playing in the barn where all of the haying equipment was stored, the barn their mother had told them not to play in. There amongst the round baler, the rake, and the swather had been an old bike covered in cobwebs, slowly rusting away. The barn was full of such junk. The nearest dump was a half hour drive away. Things that couldn't be consumed by fire in the big burning barrel behind the house were hidden out of sight in out of the way places where they could collect dust and be forgotten.

The once shiny red and white paint had faded to a dull brick color with dark cream highlights. The handlebars stood naked with no hand grips. The chain was rusted, immovable to even the hardest of cranks. The tires were rotted away, slowly breaking up, the pieces carried off by rodents. The pedals were missing, scavenged long ago to make another bike more complete. The firm rubber seat had fallen apart, leaving only the metal frame beneath. Flecks of rust covered the bike, the first signs of decay caused by the disease of time. People can borrow Mother Nature's resources as they wish, but in the end she always reclaims what is her own.

The boys had been amazed by their find. They had never noticed before this visage of a bygone time. Whose bike had it been? Who had been the boy who had once pedaled it madly, pretending to be a cowboy chasing after Indians, a knight on his mighty steed, or an American GI riding his motorcycle to glory and victory? The boys had run back to the house to ask their mother, and in their excitement forgot to hide that they had been where they were not supposed to be. The tongue lashing was quick and to the point, no time wasted on niceties. She then answered their questions. The bike had been their father's, when he was a kid.

It was a strange sensation. The boys ranked in age 13, 10, and 8. It was weird to imagine their father, a man who seemed like a giant, a man who spent the majority of his day in quiet stoicism, laughing and screaming like a lunatic as he rode his bike at breakneck speeds, playing the same games they themselves enjoyed on their own bikes. Was it so fantastic? So peculiar to imagine such a thing? To picture the man that was their father without the lines of life covering his face. Free of worries, doubts, and failures. To imagine their father entirely carefree without any responsibilities.

For the boys their bikes were everything. They were the best toy each had ever had. No other toy could be so many different things. No other toy gave them the freedom to ride out as far as they wished, to explore the world around them. No other toy allowed them to experience the risk of riding at as fast they could, feeling the wind blowing in their faces. No other toy gave them the sense of accomplishment of topping out a steep hill, sweat covering their brows, knowing they had done something they had once thought impossible. To the boys, the thought of their precious bikes rotting away in some barn under a pile of dust and spider webs was unfathomable and horrifying. Bikes were not inert objects, they were loyal steeds. They deserved a better fate than to be left uncared for and forgotten.

It's hard to say where and how ideas get formed. Time makes memories fuzzy, and pride insists that each brother remember that they were the one to come up with the original idea. Who knows how these things really happen. One likely said something. That something sparked an idea in another's mind. More words poured out, more thoughts, all building up to the big culmination. The bike was old and eroded, but it was not yet too far gone. It could be repaired. It could be fixed. The boys all shared the same thought. How would it feel to see their own bikes in such a state? How would it feel to have them restored back to their former glory? They all wanted their father to have that feeling. They could imagine their father's joy as though it was their own. A plan had begun to take shape.

They couldn't have done it on their own of course. They needed the help of an accomplice. Someone with access to tools, a car to get to town, and of course the most important thing, money. Their mother had made a most willing conspirator. For two months the boys labored secretly, braving the crisp early winter cold to sneak up to the barn and work on the old rusty bike. They worked short stints in the afternoon after they got home from school and longer stints on the weekends when their father didn't need their help.

The bike was disassembled and the frame and parts that could be salvaged were sanded until all traces of rust, grease, and dirt had been removed. Measurements were made. Lists compiled. A slight detour was added the next time their mother took a trip to town to buy groceries. New inner tubes went into new tires which went onto old frames with freshly tightened spokes. New grips, black, were placed over the bare piping of the handlebars. New pedals were attached. A new chain, freshly greased. A fresh batch of red paint on the frame and fenders, and white paint on the rims and chain guard. Sprays of WD 40 removed the squeaks of moving parts long left stationary.

The only piece of the bike that was left the way it was found was the bare rusty frame of the seat. The boys were unable to remove the old seat, which was okay given they had been unable to procure a new seat at their small town hardware store. Some sand paper and elbow grease had been applied to try and improve its look, but in the end, it was left largely as it had been found.

The boys had always made sure to work together on the project. If one brother could not join in the excursions up to the barn, work was paused until they were able. Sometimes the boys got into disagreements or bickered. It was usually over something fairly unimportant. Who got to do which task. Who was actually strong enough to loosen a nut. Sometimes the bickering would collapse into actual fighting with yelling and wrestling on the hard dirt floor until, fed up, one brother or another would rush down to tell their mother. Efforts would stop for the day, to give time for hot heads to regain their composure. Regardless, work continued and progress was made.

The holiday season came and the last coats of paint dried slowly in the cold weather. The bike was completed on time. It was magnificent. It was a work of art. It was a bike that had been restored by a bunch of kids who didn't really know what they were doing. Secrecy was of course of the essence. Their father had never gone up to the barn the entire time. The equipment stored there would not be needed until next summer. On Christmas Eve, while their father was away doing his daily chores, the bike was sneaked down to the garage, and cleverly hidden behind the various garage junk. The boys could hardly wait for the unveiling of their pride and joy.

The boys' father walked back down the driveway. He moved around the house without looking into the windows, heading straight from the front gate to the back door. The boys shook with anticipation, their excitement barely contained. They could hear him rustling in the laundry room, removing his winter gear; his coat, hat, and gloves. The back door opened and he came into the house wearing just an old t-shirt and his white cotton long underwear. He went to the kitchen and poured himself the remainder of the pot of coffee. The boys sat with their eyes glued to the kitchen doorway, waiting for him to round the corner. Every heartbeat seemed to take a minute, every minute seemed to take an hour. He walked in with his head down, studying the paper from the day before.

"Surprise!"

His head jerked up at his progeny's exclamation. His eyes sucked in the world around him.

"What's this?"

The wave of childish jubilation broke over him again.

"Your old bike, we fixed it up for you!"

He looked at the bike, studied it, and put a big grin on his face.

"Why, why that's great."

The boys were nearly jumping with joy.

"Do you like it?"

He folded up his newspaper and put it under his arm, his smile stubbornly holding on.

"Of course I do. Thank you."

The boys looked at their father expectantly. Seemingly unsure what to do, he repeated himself.

"Thank you. Thank you very much."

The boys grinned all the wider.

"Do you really like it Dad?"

The boys missed the secret smile that their mother shot over their heads. Their father ran a hand through his thinning hair.

"Yes, yes it's just wonderful."

The boys and their father were quickly gathered around the bike so a picture could be taken. The flash of the camera dazzled all of their eyes. The man looked down at his three boys looking up at him, joy and pride radiating upwards from them, watching him with expectant faces. Watching him and waiting, hoping to see the reaction that they know they themselves would have. Waiting to see their father overcome with joy and happiness. The man looked down at the bike with a critical eye, and then back at his sons again.

"You boys did a good job."

The young faces broke into even wider smiles. No one seemed sure what to do next. The man put down his coffee. He wheeled the bike out the front door, and then went back through the kitchen to put on his winter gear. The boys gathered at the big front window as the man rounded the house and wheeled the bike up the driveway. He climbed on and started to ride back and forth. The boys laughed hysterically at the giant on the tiny bike, his knees kicking up even with his eyeballs. After about five minutes their father got off and wheeled the bike down to the garage, leaving it parked next to the boys' bikes. He came back in and they all ate breakfast.

That was the only time the boys' father rode the bike. It sat in the garage and gathered dust and cobwebs. The boys rode it a few times, but it was not as good as their ten speeds, and soon it was left alone. After a time the bike was taken back up to the barn, and placed back in its corner, where its restoration slowly gave way to its former state of rust. Nobody seemed to mind.

# Giggles

Something snaps. It's hard to say exactly what it is. We've been up to this point so many times before. Brushing against the edges of the stratosphere. Not this time. No this time we rocket forward into the void. Into the unknown. One moment we are sitting on the couch, leaning together and talking, just as we always do. The next, we are tightly entwined in each other's arms, our wine and beer forgotten. Kissing. Kissing hard. Trying to entwine ourselves in an intense outburst of rampant hormones and unvoiced attraction.

I've never made a secret of it. I've never tried to hide things on my end. She's always been the one to hold back. She's always been the one to pull back when I tried to kiss her. But not tonight. Tonight there has been a lightning strike and we have become fused. She lies back on the couch and I follow her down. Our mouths explore the lips of the other, our tongues dart back forth, briefly wrestling before retreating. Her lips, her neck, her ears. All are fair game, all are open. One hand clutches her back while the other runs through dyed red hair. She closes her eyes, breathes in deep, and lets out a slight moan.

I feel myself stiffen, pressing against the denim layer of my jeans.

She is Giggles, a silly name earned by the fits of laughter she couldn't suppress from the first time we made out, the first time we really hung out. It had been a strange ridiculous night. Sitting and talking, joking in a bar over beers and shots. Going back to her place to try freshly made Jello shots. Dancing without any music playing. A sudden kiss. A sudden movement. Rolling on the floor kissing. She had suddenly stopped. She had started giggling uncontrollably. What could I do? I could either sit there awkwardly or I could laugh as well. I chose the option that was less awkward.

I am her cabana boy. A joke from the bar the same night when she earned her name. What do I want to do when I get out of graduate school? What do I want to be when I finally stop delaying the start of my life? I don't want a real job. I don't want to be another starched shirt in an office. I'll be a cabana boy. I'll get a tan and wear short shorts. I'll laze off. I'll serve fruity drinks with umbrellas and flirt outrageously with women above my social standing. I don't want to be responsible. I don't want a real life. I just want to live ridiculous.

We're no longer on the couch. I'm not sure how we got here, but somehow we are on the floor. How did we completely miss the coffee table? I don't have time to really question the mysteries of life. I'm too busy blowing in the storm that has engulfed us. We had just been talking, talking like we always do. It had become the norm. I call and come over. We talk, joke, and have a good time. I try to kiss her. She pulls back. We talk more. I try to kiss her again. She pulls back. It gets awkward. I go home. Not this time. No, not this time. My hand runs up underneath her shirt. It grips her breast, teasing her small pink nipple between my fingers. I pull her shirt up and lower my head.

Confused. So confused. Some days she's hot, other days she's cold. She's my best friend. She's probably the first person that I've managed to let in this far. We talk often, about everything and anything. We talk about happy times and bad times, joy and despair, hopes and dreams. We talk about ridiculous things. We make up silly stories that leave us both in fits of laughter. But I don't share all of myself. I don't let out everything that I am. There is so much of my life that feels like nothing more than an act. A show put on so that I can find myself in these situations. I've been alone for so long. I don't feel like people will want to be with the person I am inside.

We often talk about sex. She talks about her inexperience. She talks about her ex, her one and only boyfriend. She talks about how he never gave her an orgasm. I am experienced in all of these things, or at least so I claim, not a virgin, but I've never had anything close to what could be called a relationship. I've always had a yearning. I've always been lonely. I have a knowledge of sex and intimacy comparable to a sixteen year old boy. I do what I feel like I have to. I lie. I pretend I know so much more than I actually do. I pretend that I know what's going on and how the world works. Sometimes she asks me about my dick. So I tell her, a rare completely honest truth.

My hand snakes from her breast and moves along her belly. It begins to move below her belt, softly tugging to move it free. She grabs my hand and brings it upward. Again my hand maneuvers its way downward. Again she grabs it and moves it back.

"I want to fuck you. I want you so bad."

"It's not going to happen."

We do not break our embrace. Our words are muttered out between kisses and our mouths moving to explore other parts of our upper bodies.

"Why not?"

"I…..I haven't cleaned myself up down there. I don't want you to see it."

"I don't care."

"No, not tonight."

We continue to caress and explore. The intensity in no way lessened by our exchange of words. Our bodies began to run on automatic. My stiffness bulges against my pants, demanding attention, demanding release. My hips begin to spasm and rock in the timeless precursor called dry humping. Her hips rise to meet mine and they convulse together. Both our bodies yearn for the connection of the other. I can feel the heat of her, I can feel her need rising like mine as she involuntarily moans.

She pulls away. She gets up and pulls her shirt down. For a moment her eyes meet mine with an intense desire. She breaks the gaze and looks away. I lay on my side and watch her. She walks over to a shelf and lights several candles. She walks over to the switch next to the door and turns off the light. The room is plunged into fluttering darkness. Her eyes flick to mine and away as I watch her. Dancing shadows roam back and forth on the walls. She comes towards me and pushes me on to my back. She is a small woman, but I let her. I am powerless to do anything else. She unbuttons my pants and pulls them downward. I raise my hips and help pull them down to my ankles. Her hand grips my shaft and tugs at it. She looks me in the eye. Her voice is just a whisper.

"Just lay there, don't jerk or thrust."

I nod my understanding and her head drops. Her mouth envelopes my erection. Her hand cups my balls as the other tugs at the base of my shaft. Her head moves up and down in a constant motion, stopping from time to time only to lick the length of it or to play with my urethra with the tip of her tongue. I sit back and enjoy it as much as I can, the excitement of the moment drowning out my worries over what the hell is going on. My mind doesn't have time to worry. It's all so sudden, so new, so much like a dream come true.

I want to watch. I want to see. I want her eyes to meet mine. I want to see her do her magical work. I try to pull her hair back so I can see. She pushes my arm back to the ground beside me and lets her hair fall back, a protective cocoon that hides her from the judging world. I convulse and jerk. I'm getting close. I'm about to explode. My voice is strained by my ecstasy,

"I'm coming, I'm coming."

She does not pull back, she draws me in deeper and increases her pace. My hips convulse again. My seed erupts from me in great spurts into her mouth. She swallows them, taking all that I have to give. I fall back, spent and tired. She does not stop. She continues her rapid motions. A runner that has crossed the finish line but continues moving forward. I push slightly on her shoulder.

"I'm done. I'm done. You can stop."

She pulls back and looks away from me. I look at her, she continues to stare at the floor. The intensity is gone, the flow of hormones is missing. It's just us again. She looks at me through her mussed up hair and I see vulnerability and fear. Worries and hard self-judgment. I see a mind that that is unsure and desperately trying to figure out what to do now. Her eyes mirror my own.

I stand up, pull up, and rebutton my pants. I can't stay. I'm afraid. I'm scared to death. What am I doing? Walk over, pull her up, take her in your arms. Hold her, carry her back to the bedroom. Ravish her. Comfort her. Make her feel like everything is all right. Make her feel like this changes nothing, that we are still the same people. Make her feel like it was not a bad decision. Let her know that this can be the start of a good thing. Say something. Say anything.

There is nobody there to do the same for me. I'm scared. I'm frightened. I'm unsure. I don't know what I'm doing. I don't know for sure what I want. I don't know what all of this means. I don't know where we go from here. I'm so scared. I don't say anything. We just stare at one another, both hoping that the other can be brave, that the other is strong enough and confident enough. I grab my hat and coat from where I left them on the floor. I turn and I do not look back. I flee. I run away. I feel her frightened eyes on me as the door closes behind me.

My phone rings. I pause the movie I'm watching and pick it up.

"Hello."

"Hi."

The voice on the other end is one I recognize. One that is embedded in my memory. The voice is slurred. Giggles has been drinking. It's only nine o'clock here, which means it's only eight o'clock in northern Idaho. How in the hell did she manage to get so drunk this early in the evening on a Sunday? Beneath the tones of alcohol are others, more subtle. Nervousness with just a hint of desperation.

"Hey, how are you doing?"

"I'm good."

Her words are drawn out, as though she's avoiding pushing them forward. I can picture her in my mind as she must be on the other end of the phone. Rounded cheek and pointed chin. Her blonde hair, dyed red, slightly ruffled and out of place. Her eyes, slightly out of focus from the booze, staring off at a distant wall, willing away self-doubt. Her small hands softly caressing her neck and occasionally twirling a loose strand of hair around a finger.

"What about you?"

"I'm good too. Just sitting around lazing off. What's up?"

I don't know why I rush through the small talk. I really am doing nothing. Just working my way through a stack of rented movies. I don't know why I'm hurrying to get back to them. There is little enough to do around here.

The other end is silent for a moment. I can hear her breathing as she collects her thoughts. The wind whistles around the walls of my house. It's springtime according to the calendar, but according to the temperature and the snow, it's still winter. I'm beginning to believe that it's always going to be winter in Canada.

"I'm not going to be able to come visit you. I still haven't found a job and I don't have enough money."

"Oh. Don't worry about it. That's okay."

"Are you sure?"

"Of course, if you don't have the money, you don't have the money."

I mean what I say. I am disappointed. I had been looking forward to her driving north for a visit. There isn't a lot to do in these god forsaken prairies, especially if you're a man who doesn't really know anybody and has trouble forcing himself out of his comfort zone. The kind of man who instead of making new friends overwhelms other fears to pick up a phone and call someone they haven't talked to in months. Someone who seemed to want nothing to do with him. Someone who in the past he's only returned reaching out with silence, until somehow magically they pick up the phone, start talking, and make plans. Plans that aren't going to happen now. It's all right. But it's just one of those things. You can't really get mad or depressed about it. It's one of those things that are completely out of your control. She doesn't have the money to come up, and I don't have the money to offer to pay to get her up here. Such is life.

"I wish I could come up."

"I wish you could too."

"Maybe I can figure something out."

"Don't worry about it."

Silence again. I hear a deep sigh before the slurring voice returns. I can tell by the sound of her voice that her eyes are getting cloudy.

"I just wanted to come up and visit you so bad."

"I know. I know. Don't worry about it."

Again, just the sound of breathing. The quiet drags on too long. I begin to wonder if I should say something to break the silence. Say something so it doesn't get uncomfortable. Finally she speaks again. Her voice quiet, almost a whisper.

"Can I tell you something?"

"Yeah."

"Are you sure?"

"Yeah, you can tell me anything."

A pause. She sucks in a breath. It comes out in a whispered slurry rush.

"Sometimes I look at your pictures on Facebook."

I don't know what to say. It's something everybody does. We all have looked at other people's pictures. Sometimes because we have a crush, sometimes because we despise them, sometimes just because we're curious to look into the window at their lives. We all do it, but it's something else to have somebody actually admit to doing it to yours. The silence is too long, her voice gains a panicked edge.

"Maybe I shouldn't have said that."

I let out a quick snorted chuckle.

"No, no, it's all right. To be honest, I've looked at your photos on Facebook too."

"Really?"

"Yeah."

It's the truth. I find her attractive in a way I find hard to explain. She isn't the prettiest woman in the world. She's short and round. But there's something about her, there's something about her that draws me in. Maybe it's just that we both always seemed slightly out of place in the world. Two people who never seemed like they quite fit. I don't know. Some people stick in your mind more than others. Some people just heat you up easier than others. I have looked at her pictures on Facebook before. Hell, I've even masturbated to them from time to time. I don't mention this last part. I can only reveal so much of the truth at one time. My admitting to the same shameful sin as herself has made us co-conspirators. I can hear a little less nervousness in her drunken voice.

"Do you like what you see?"

I smile to myself.

"Yes, yes I do."

I feel a sudden urge to tell her more of the truth. A sudden urge to tell her I think about her a lot. To tell her that sometimes I think about that night long ago. That sometimes I look at her pictures, my heart pounding in my ears, my dick in my hand, and imagine all the dirty things I'd like to do to her. I stifle it. There is a time and place for everything, and right now is not the time to start pouring out my heart. I imagine her smiling to herself on the other end. Maybe she is having some of the exact same thoughts that I am. The thought makes me excited. The voice on the other end gets wistful again.

"God I wish I could come up to visit you."

"Me too."

"What would we do?"

"We'd go to the dinosaur museum and drive out to Calgary. We'd have a lot of fun."

"This sucks."

"Yeah."

Silence again. Even over the phone I can feel something building. She's drunk, her lips are loose, just loose enough to let some things usually held in slip out.

"I love you."

I don't know what to say. The bluntness and blatantness of the statement throws me back a step. Something that I had never had the guts to do. I don't know what to say. I just sit there, like an idiot. Her voice breaks the silence, the nervousness has returned as well as a touch of fear.

"Is that all right?"

"Yeah. Yeah. It's all right."

I can feel my words get swallowed into the void. I lick my lips and try to think what to say. For a second I can feel an echo of her words start to worm their way from my brain to my mouth. The words are on the tip of my tongue. I've never heard someone outside of my immediate family tell me that before. I've never said those words intimately to anyone. I am a sixteen year old trapped in a twenty-six year old's body. I try to spit them out, but I can't. The words don't come.

"Well...."

She pauses unsure what to do now that her confession has left her lips. Unsure what to do now that the conversation has gotten awkward. The words become rushed.

"Well, I better get going."

My words are rushed too. The awkwardness is uncomfortable for both of us.

"Yeah. No problem. I'll talk to you later."

"Yeah, talk to you later."

"Bye."

"Bye."

The phone goes dead. I put it down and lean back in my chair. I stare out the window at the small flakes swirling in the wind outside my window. There is a sense of elation deep inside of me. A sense of pride that someone would say such words to me. There is a sense of disappointment. I feel like a coward. I should have been able to say it back. Confusion. How do I feel? Yes, I think about her, but does that necessarily mean I love her? Do I think about her because I love her, or because she was the last one that I thought I might have feelings for?

It's strange to think about. All the impulses that enter our minds, how we act on some while others are ignored. It had been an impulse. An impulse to call her and talk to her. The first time in more than a year. I had been heading north after spending New Year's with friends in Boise. I was heading north to go back to work. Where she lived was on the way. It had just been an impulse. An impulse to pick up my phone. An impulse that had led to having lunch together. An impulse that led to phone calls back and forth. An impulse that had led to plans to come up and visit me. An impulse that had led to the phone conversation tonight. I sit in my chair and watch the snow, not knowing what to think or how to feel.

The winters in Alberta are brutal, but the early summer is beautiful. Never too hot. Gentle summer breezes coursing through the trees. Perfect summer day follows perfect summer day, week after week. The yard of the house that I rent has never been well taken care of. What was mostly likely once a yard of grass is now several years worth of dead and rotting leaves beneath gnarled and unkempt trees. Patches of grass survive here and there along the perimeter and in small islands where the sunshine still breaks through. Creeping vines mount an attack upon the foundation along the side of the house.

Every weekend I head out into this untamed wilderness to do battle. The mistakes of the past have piled up with no attempts to repair them until now. It will take some time to rectify them. Today has been especially slow, digging up networks of vines that have set their roots deep. Even in the cool shade along the side of the house I sweat. My work is slowed by my neighbor constantly trying to start up conversations. He's a nice enough man, but strange. He's short and squat, reminding me of an obese hobbit. He always has a can of Molson beer in his hand. He never wears a shirt, something that seems much too common in a country where it gets so cold. My neighbor is a friendly welcoming man. I'm cold and distant. I have a hard time making friends, and I don't really want to be his friend.

I hear the phone ring through the open window. I push my shovel into the newly bared dirt and run around to the back door, kicking my feet against the frame to knock any loose dirt off my leather work boots. I reach the phone by the fourth ring. I feel a sense of pride wash over me at making it so quickly, as though someone else was keeping track of my amazing phone answering skills.

"Hello."

"Hi."

I recognize the distant voice on the other end. "Hey, how are you?"

"Fine. How about you?"

"Doing good."

It has been two and a half months since I've heard from her. Only silence since the strange drunken call. I don't really know what to do or how to react. I can feel a thrill run, through me. I've been hoping she'd call, but I don't know what to say. I decide to try to be cool and play it by ear.

"What's new down in Idaho?"

"Not much. Still living with my parents and looking for a job."

"That's too bad. I haven't had much to do at work lately. Weather's been pretty nice. I've been working out in the yard all day."

"That sounds like fun."

Sarcasm.

"Oh yeah, just a blast."

More sarcasm.

"How's the weather been down there?"

"Warming up pretty fast."

I can feel that it's a little awkward, navigating these niceties, these social graces. I've never been one for such things. I find them boring, but they make a nice cover to avoid talking about more uncomfortable things. A few more back and forths take place, catching both of us up on the small minute changes that take place in one's life over eight weeks. Slowly but surely we run out of things to say, the pauses grow longer, the elephant in the room looms larger, just waiting for someone to point it out. She loses her nerve before I do.

"I'm sorry for being so drunk last time we talked."

"That's all right."

"You probably think I said a lot of strange stuff."

"It's okay. I feel the same way about you."

It comes out of my mouth before I even realize it. An escapee who has somehow avoided the filter between brain and tongue. I try to bite it back, but it's too late, it's already out there. I brace myself. There is a short silence. I hear an intake of breath on the other end of the phone.

"Really?"

There's no use in denying it now. The box has been opened. There's no going back.

"Yeah really."

"Me too."

I can hear the excitement in her voice, stifled slightly by the holding back of things long gone unsaid.

"I worried that you didn't. I worried that you were still mad about what happened?"

"What happened?"

"That night in my apartment back in Moscow. You know, when we...... Then you just left and didn't say anything. I was worried that I did something wrong. I was worried that you were mad at me."

"No. I wasn't mad. Just scared and confused."

"I know it must have been confusing for you. I was always you know..... It was........ it was just that I was so horny that night. I don't know what came over me. Then you just got up and left without saying anything. I felt like I must have done something wrong."

"You did nothing wrong. I shouldn't have left. I should have stayed. But I was scared."

"I didn't know what to think."

"I shouldn't have left. I've regretted it for a long time. I should have stayed there."

"I worried that maybe you didn't like it. That maybe I sucked at giving head."

I smile to myself. The conversation has brought back memories and my body is starting to react to them.

"No, it was a great blowjob. One of the best ones I've ever had."

"Really?"

"Yeah."

It's an easy call to make, I haven't had that many blowjobs. Her voice goes low and comes out like the purr of a cat.

"I wish I could give you another one."

"Me too."

"That and more. Can I tell you something?"

"Sure."

"I've never had an orgasm during sex. Just during masturbation. Do you think that's weird?"

"No. Maybe you just haven't had the right man."

I try to sound confident, like I know what I'm talking about. I've only had sex twice in my entire life. It's not something I want people to know. I always try to sound like I know more and have done more than I actually do or have done. A significant portion of sixteen year olds know more about sex than I do. I haven't done anything with anyone in more than a year.

"When I masturbate I always lay on my belly, it's the only way I can get off."

"Have you ever been taken from behind?"

"What?"

"You know, doggy-style. Maybe that would do it?"

"Oh."

Silence. Maybe I said something wrong. Her sultry voice returns.

"Tell me how big it is again."

The question is not unusual. I can remember many questions such as this back when we were in college. A glint in her eyes, a look of pleasure on her face for being dirty, her tongue lightly licking her upper lip.

"Six and a half inches."

"So big. God I'm horny."

At least I know she hasn't seen a lot of dicks.

"Me too."

"Have you ever tried phone sex?"

"No."

Silence. "Would you like to?"

I can feel myself bulge against my dirt covered jeans. My hand has been unconsciously rubbing myself for some time now.

"Yeah. Yeah I'd love to. I don't know how we get started."

"I don't know."

"Maybe tell me what you're doing right now."

"I'm laying on my bed. I'm wearing just a t-shirt and sweatpants, no bra. I can feel my nipples growing harder."

I walk into my bedroom and close the door behind me. I undo my pants and pull them down around my ankles before sitting against the wall. I put my phone in my left hand and rub myself with my right as I listen to her talk.

"I'm so horny. I want you so bad…….Okay, now it's your turn."

"I come up behind you and kiss your neck. One hand reaches up underneath your shirt and fondles your breast. I can feel the heat coming off of you. My other hand rubs around your waist band and then snakes downward, lightly rubbing your twat."

Her breathing on the phone gets heavier. I can see her in my mind's eye, face down on her bed, rubbing herself.

"I'm so wet. I want you right now."

"I pull down your sweats. You're not wearing any panties. I put my fingers inside of you and bend you over on the bed. I pull your shirt up to reveal your perky nipples and then slide my throbbing dick into you."

Her voice is a heavy pulsing whisper.

"Yes. Yes. Are you fucking me?"

I can feel my own excitement rise. My voice lowers, its cadence matching the rhythm of my hand.

"I begin to move in and out of you. In and out. I begin to slowly speed up, holding your hips with my hands."

I hear a moan on the other side of the phone.

"One finger."

"In and out. Faster and faster. You push yourself back into me, wanting me deeper inside of you. Your arms can no longer hold you up, your front falls, your head pushes down into the mattress. I start to fuck you harder. My dick going deeper with every thrust. Your body convulsing with every inward and outward stroke."

Her breathing grows more rapid. Every exhale accentuated with the involuntary sound of pleasure.

"Fuck me. Fuck me harder. Two fingers."

I can see her, lying on her belly, both hands underneath her, one inside, one rubbing her clit. Her face is contorted in painful pleasure. The thought makes me harder. I begin to have trouble containing my own excitement.

"Harder and deeper. Harder and deeper. You feel weak. Your legs give out and you collapse beneath me, but I just fuck you harder. I can feel your pleasure building. You want to cum don't you?"

"Oh god yes."

I rub my shaft faster and faster. Increasing the tempo of my imaginary thrusting.

"Harder and deeper. I'm a fucking machine. You can feel yourself on the edge. Part of you wants me to stop, to let you pull back from the brink. Part of you wants to take a flying leap over the cliff. Faster. Harder. Deeper."

"Oh god. Oh god! Oh god!!"

Her voice rises. I can see her convulse with the power of her orgasm. A wave of confidence and accomplishment washes over me. I feel like I am a god. I feel like I can do anything. My own pleasure reaches the tipping point and hot white ejaculate sprays out, covering my pants and my hand. We both sit in silence, listening to the heavy breathing of the other. Coming down from the heights. She is the first to speak.

"That was amazing."

"God yes."

"Can we do it again sometime?"

"Of course. Anytime you want."

We talk a bit more, the memories of our words lost by the much larger memory of what we had just done. Finally we make our goodbyes and I hang up the phone. I sit against the wall of my room, letting the last ripples of euphoria flow over me, and then clean myself up with a dirty sock lying nearby. I zip up and rebutton my pants, and then go back outside to finish my work eradicating the vines.

I stand in the front yard. The morning is cold for August. I watch her car pull away down the street, turn a corner and disappear. The grass and street are damp. The world still smells of the summer rain that cleansed the world just a few hours ago. The first few drops of a second storm begin to fall, little spots of darkness on the light gray of the sidewalk. The air smells fresh and new, cleansed by the falling water. I wish the rain could cleanse me of my sins.

I'm having a hard time wrapping my brain around everything that has happened. I feel dirty, rotten, like filth. I am a shining knight no more. I have shed my armor and crawled down into the pit with the squalid masses. I am no better than them. I am one of them. In the narration of your life you can talk yourself up until you stand high above the rest, but in the end it is one's actions that decide one's placement in this world. The rain begins to fall heavier. These summer storms are fast and furious. I turn and walk into the house.

I have lived in this house for only about a month, and I can already tell that it will never feel like a home. The house is filled by another person's things, the owners, someone willing to rent a room to his friend's wife's cousin. My small room is a miniscule bastion of me in a sea of him. Television, video game console, dresser, small twin bed, and beer making equipment. I don't own much. I've been travelling fairly light. Each move results in fewer and fewer belongings. Each move gets easier and easier.

I flop down on my bed and try not to think about the past few days. The bed has some comfort to it beyond the mattress and blankets. It's the top half of my childhood bunk bed. It's easy to take apart and easy to move. It's a ridiculous bed for a twenty-six year old man to be sleeping on. Guilt. I feel nothing but guilt and regret. The more I try to not think about it, the more it fills my mind. My body begins to shake. Desperation. I have to do something to fix this. There is nothing I can do. Only turn away and try to move forward with my life. Guilt. So much guilt.

The numbers on the alarm clock are flashing. The power must have blinked, or perhaps my roommate/landlord popped the fuse again. I pick up the black box and reset the clock. Each click brings things back to where they should be. It's like travelling through time. I wish I could travel through time. Travel back and fix things. Make things better. I can't. I'm stuck here. I don't know what to do. I don't know how to move forward. I would give anything to make things better. To remove the hurt that I have caused. Nothing. Nothing can be done.

I open the front door. She stands in the doorway, smiling, cheerful despite the six hour car drive. I smile back. We hug. The feel of her bare arms on my neck. I haven't seen her in person in eight months. The sky is filled with clouds. Maybe it will rain. Awkwardness. I don't know what to say or do. I feel excited. Nervous. Her body shakes a little. We separate. She's nervous too. She picks up her bag and comes inside. I lead her back to my room. Her eyes drink everything in. We sit down on the bed to catch up. She looks giddy. I can't stop smiling. She pulls out a photo album. She tells me she plans on filling it with pictures from the trip. She's always been artsy. I'm glad that she's here.

I've only been here for a month. I'd been offered a good job. I'd taken it. No more Canada. Closer to my family. A good deal. No closer to her. Just a different direction. It had been a big change. When I was a kid this city had always been the big city. A place full of people who looked down on their so-called bumpkin rural neighbors. Before here the biggest city I had ever lived in had been twenty-five thousand people. Aside from my roommate, I really don't know anyone. He's not the type I really want to hang out with. The word of god is constantly on his lips.

Giggles coming to visit had been a wonderful surprise. Something familiar in this strange new world. It had happened during a phone conversation. I had thrown out the bait, not expecting any bites. We could go downtown and see the city, explore some of the museums, go to the zoo. The zoo was the worm that caught the fish. Weeks of waiting. Weeks of excitement. No one but my parents had ever gone to such lengths just to see me. My mind had run wild with expectations.

"What about the zoo? When can we go to the zoo?"

"Tomorrow. I figured tonight we'd ride the train downtown to get dinner and a couple of drinks."

She smiles.

"Okay."

We ride the train downtown. Her eyes stay glued on the view outside. My gaze sticks to her. We get out and she stares upward at the buildings towering above us.

"How can you live here? It all feels so big. I don't think I could find my way around."

Her words sound hickish in my ears.

"You get used to it. Figure out things as you go."

I'm nervous. The night is cool but I can still feel droplets of sweat dribble down my back. We walk hand in hand, pointing out the various stores that we could walk into if they weren't closed for the night. I want to grab her. I want to pull her in close. I want to kiss her. But I don't. I'm nervous. I'm scared. I'm frightened. Why am I so nervous? Why am I so scared? It seems like something that should be easy. This is a woman who has told me she loves me. This is a woman that I've told that I love. I fret as we walk. What is wrong with me? I don't feel like I should kiss her. I don't feel like she wants me to. This is not what I expected. This is not what I was looking forward to. Are these vibes real, do they represent truly how she feels, or are they just self-doubt?

I steer us into a local bar, one of the few that I know in the city. Maybe some liquid courage will help give me the steely reserve I need. Quell my overactive brain. Let me relax. Let me be myself. We sit at a table with our beers and talk over the blare of an Irish jig band which plays from a stage in the corner.

I talk about the foibles of adjusting to life here and why I left Canada. She talks about getting a new job and moving to Boise, hanging out with her roommate and their new friend Corey.

Every time I stop talking I take a drink of beer. Something to give an excuse to the silence. I don't hear well in crowded rooms. At some points I can't make out what she says. Sometimes I ask her to repeat herself. Most of the time I just politely nod. The drinks of beer add up. Conversations in a crowded noisy bar have lots of silences. By the time we get up to leave I pay for five beers. She's only had one.

We walk around the city a bit more. The beer has gone straight to my head. We look for a place to eat but I get us lost. We end up in the more run down part of downtown. The area where bums sleep in doorways and prod people for change. The streets are dirty and so are the people. This city is not a dangerous place, but I can tell that it makes her nervous.

We find a place to eat and I have another two beers with dinner. She has none. She grows more distant. She's tired, it's been a long trip. I do not act like myself. I become boastful and talk only about myself. My mind is on one thing and one thing only. I don't care about the rest. I'm not cognizant enough to understand the problem. She grows more distant and I get more nervous and try harder, making her more distant. I'm desperate to reverse the problem and only make it worse. Finally she says she's tired and we ride the train back home. I'm drunk and unsure of myself. The ride back is uncomfortably silent.

We get back to the house. She goes into the bathroom to get changed into shorts and shirt to sleep in. I peel off all my clothes, but my underwear, and slip underneath the covers. She comes in, turns out the light, and gets into bed next to me. It's a tight fit. It's been a long time. I'm twenty-six and I have only had sex twice in my entire life. The thought of sex is a thought of desperation, a thought that overrides all others. My hand reaches over and grabs her breast. She bats it away. I sit up and try to kiss her. She reciprocates, but then she pushes me away. I feel puzzled, confused. I lean in to kiss her again. She starts to reciprocate. I hear heavy breathing. My excitement rises. She pushes me away again.

I push back, pushing down with my weight, and kiss her hard on the mouth. She pushes back harder and we break apart again. My brain feels sluggish, my thoughts are cloudy. I'm unsure what to think or feel. I look down at her and see the fear in her eyes. I see how scared she is. The cogs of my brain start to catch up with my actions. My own needs and wants fizzle and disappear. Waves of guilt pass over me. Dizzy. Scared. The world is swirling around me. My body collapses next to hers on the tiny twin mattress. She's breathing deeply. She's afraid. I try to think of something to say, something to fix the harm that I've done, but nothing comes out. My thoughts wade through a swamp of alcohol. The darkness claims me.

The next morning we barely talk. I don't know what to say. The brightness of day brings clarity, but it does little to help the problem. We go and eat breakfast at Dennys. We sit quietly, staring at each other. When we get back in her car I try to apologize. Try to tell her how sorry I am. She just looks at me, her eyes filled with fear and sadness. Her voice is barely a whisper.

"I think it's best if I go home."

She drops me off at the house, grabs her bag from my room, and drives away. I lay on my bed for most of the day, horrified at the thing that I've done. I feel sick. I feel like I need to puke. Her eyes hang in my mind, filled with fear and sadness. Asking why. Why are you acting like this? Why are you hurting me? Why? My body starts shaking. I stare at the wall until it stops. I sit all day and desperately try to figure out what to do. Desperately try to think of some solution that will make this all go away. Something that will fix this. There is none. There is no way to take back the actions that created last night. There is nothing to take away her fear. I don't want to be me. I don't want last night to have happened. I don't know what to do.

How could I do this? How could I scare somebody so badly? It doesn't make sense. I'm scared of the world. I'm scared of everything. How can a person like me scare someone else? What have I done? I'm a monster. I'm a fucking monster. No. Yes. I'm the worst possible person. She looked so scared. So frightened. How could I do that to her? What must she be feeling right now? Six hours. A six hour car drive. Scared to death. Fuck. Fuck me. I don't deserve to live. I hope I die. Good god please let me just die.

You get up. You shower. You eat. You go to work. You come home. You sleep. Repetitiveness. Every day the same as the last. Things move from the present into the past. You cannot do anything to change the past, so you try to forget about it, leave it behind. You can only think about the future. You cannot change the past, but you can try and do better in the future.

I shake with nervousness as I dial the number into my phone. It has been a week. My palms are slick with sweat. The phone rings, and rings, and rings. There is no answer. The phone goes to voicemail. I hang up.

I try again a week later. Same steps. Shake with nervousness. Dial the number. The phone rings, again, and again. Nobody answers, it goes to voicemail.

"Hey it's me. I'm sorry I haven't called sooner. I just wanted to call to say how sorry I was. I feel terrible. I'm sorry. I'm so very sorry."

I feel like I should say more. I don't know what to say. I hit the button and cut off the call. What more could I add? Just more words. Nothing can make the situation any better. Nothing.

A few days later she sends me a text message.

*I'm okay. Probably better if we don't talk.*
I text back.
*Okay.*

It's not something you'll forget. It's not something that disappears. You look in the mirror and you can see her. You can see her eyes, filled with fear. What are you supposed to do? Wallow for the rest of your life? Lock yourself in your room and wait until the end? You can't do that. You have to stand up and learn to walk again. You can't start doing better if you don't start walking. Is it okay to forgive yourself? Is it enough to do everything in your power to be a better person? The months drop by. The green leaves of summer wither and fall around you, choking the sidewalks with their musty odor. The weather turns cold and gray. The world moves forward, so must you. Winter may come, but spring may come again. After a time you don't think about it every day, but you never forget. You can never let yourself forget. Any of it.

The phone rings, jolting me from my sleep. I look at the clock as I reach for it. Two-thirty in the morning on a Tuesday. Who could be calling now? The voice on the other end is one I recognize. It sounds slurred and panicked. I can tell that she's been crying.
"Hello."
"Why does this keep happening to me?"
"What?"
"Corey. Why did he act like that? Don't know what to do. He was the one who drove me here. I don't know what to do."
"Where are you?"
"I didn't think I was leading him on."
"Are you safe? Is everything okay?"
"I don't know what to do."
"Calm down. Are you in trouble? Do you need help?"

"He just got so mad, so I just walked away. I don't know what to do."

"Are you all right?"

The phone goes dead. I try to dial the number, but it just goes straight to voicemail. I don't sleep for the rest of the night. The next day I get a text message.

*Everything is all right. Sorry I bothered you.*

I text back.

*What happened?*

Silence.


Spring rains fall as I walk from the train station back to the house. Cars race down the freeway beneath me as my feet carry me across the bridge of steel and concrete. I reach the far side. My phone buzzes in my pocket. A single text. The word "Giggles" stares up at me from the phone's front screen. My stomach knots. I feel sick. I flip it open.

*How have you been?*

*I've been fine. You?*

*Good. Still in Portland?*

*Yes. Still in Boise?*

Silence. Nothing more.

# Digory

A group of us were sitting in the bar for happy hour, though the time for discounted drinks had long since passed. We sat swapping stories of bygones and funny memories, just passing the time until we felt sufficiently pickled enough to either decide what we were going to do for the rest of the evening or just go home while our minds and bodies were still able.

One friend looked at his wife, grinning like a Cheshire cat. "Honey you should tell the turtle story."

She looked back at him in mock annoyance, the kind of look that lets you know it was all a schtick they had rehearsed many times before. "I can't tell that story, it's too depressing."

"Oh c'mon, it's hilarious."

"All right, all right, fine. I'll tell it."

What follows is the story that she told.

When I was a young girl, only about ten, my father decided to get me and my brother a pet so we had something to take care of and play with. Being a smart enough man to realize that any pet he got us would ultimately end up his responsibility, he chose to forgo the usual pets, such as cats or a dogs. Fish were too boring, ponys took up too much space, and guinea pigs died so often that there was really no use in naming them. With all this in mind, he went to the pet store without telling my brother and I what he was bringing home.

The two of us were literally jumping with excitement when my father pulled into the driveway and got out of the car with something hidden under his coat. We ran up to him as he opened the front door, demanding to see what he was hiding. My father, however, was a showman. He made the whole family sit down on the couch and started the routine which he used for the presentation of all surprises. His words, using only general terms, weaved a feeling of excitement that permeated the entire room. My father had a real talent, he should have been a show hawker at a carnival. He could make the mundane seem amazing. My brother and I were soon sitting on the edge of our seats, shivering with anticipation. My mother, more immune to my father's antics, sat back with a look in her eye that suggested she needed another glass of wine. Finally, when my brother and I were about ready to explode, he took our new pet out from under his coat. It was a turtle.

By that point we would have been excited if he had brought out a house plant. We oohed and ahhed at our new pet and rattled off a thousand questions all at once.

"What does he eat?"

"Where will he live?"

"What can he do?"

"Does he know any tricks?"

My father answered each question with a deep air of knowledge and authority. By the way he talked you would have thought the man was a professional herpetologist. We kids drank it in like gospel. My mother rolled her eyes and went into the kitchen to check dinner and get the aforementioned wine. My father continued with his one man show. He went back out to the car and brought back the various supplies necessary to properly care for our new pet.

A large aquarium was to be our turtle's home, which our father proudly put on a shelf on our overly large TV stand. First went in the gravel to line the bottom, then the water. My brother and I formed a fire brigade, filling pitchers in the bathtub and bringing them out to my father who carefully dumped them into the aquarium with a great amount of ceremony. Then came the heat lamp. My father explained how the turtle was cold blooded and didn't have a constant body temperature like us warm blooded critters. Next came three large fake plastic plants, a pirate's treasure chest, and finally the turtle.

My brother and I argued over what the name of our new turtle would be. My brother wanted to name him Raphael, after his favorite Ninja Turtle. I wanted to name him Digory, after my favorite character in the Chronicles of Narnia. The debate soon got heated, which for us meant we were screaming and getting close to hitting each other. My father intervened. With great solemnity he reached into his pocket and pulled out a quarter. Heads, the name would be Raphael, tails, it would be Digory. We waited with baited breath as the quarter flipped into the air, clear to the ceiling. It seemed to move in slow motion back to the floor. I of course won the coin toss. I've always been better at coin tosses than my brother. He took it with his usual grace, insisting on calling the turtle Raphael for a few months until finally acquiescing to the rest of the family's failure to adapt to his opinion.

Digory seemed to enjoy his new home in the aquarium, swimming around and doing acrobatics to the delight of the entire family. He especially seemed to love the fake plants in his tank. He would often sit, floating in the water, his bottom legs pressed into the mass of fake plastic greenery, stretching his head to keep it above water. My brother and I fed him as we had promised to do, but most of Digory's more complicated care fell to my father. My mother did nothing with Digory, and really seemed to have no interest in changing that dynamic.

Unfortunately, as time went on, it became apparent that Digory was not a nice turtle. In fact, Digory was a bit of an asshole. Whenever we took him out of his tank to play with him he'd try to bite us, or scurry off to try and hide under the couch. Over time it got to the point where we entirely lost interest in Digory. No kid wants to play with a pet that is constantly trying to hurt them. In all fairness, Digory didn't seem to like us much either. When it came time to clean his aquarium, my father would put him in a bucket of water for safe keeping. Nearly every time Digory would somehow manage to climb out of the bucket. He would then attempt to slip past my father, who was diligently working on cleaning Digory's home, to make a scurrying escape down the driveway. He was invariably always caught. Turtles are not the fastest of animals.

Soon all of Digory's care, including feeding, fell to my father. Digory spent most of his time swimming in his aquarium and clinging to his beloved plants, completely ignored by the family except for his basic care. Twelve years passed, my brother and I graduated from high school and moved on to college. My father stayed home and took care of our not so beloved childhood pet that just wouldn't die. Apparently, nobody at the pet store had bothered informing my father about the lengthy lifespan of the average turtle. Digory was like a crotchety bachelor uncle that no one really liked, but we allowed in the house because he was family. Out of all of us, my father was the only who developed any kind of attachment to Digory, but it was probably only due to the time he'd put into taking care of the little bastard, not because of any likable qualities Digory possessed.

One day my father noticed a strange discolored patch on Digory's shell. Concerned, my father took him to the nearest veterinarian with turtle experience. The vet quickly diagnosed the problem and began quizzing my father on proper turtle care.

"Are you feeding him the proper diet?"

"Oh yes, of course, we only feed him the turtle food they sell at the pet store."

"Are keeping his tank clean?"

"Yes."

"Do you have a heat lamp with the proper wattage?"

"Of course."

"He's cold blooded you know."

"Yes, we've had him for twelve years now."

"Are you keeping the water at the proper pH levels?"

"Check it all the time."

"Is his rock of the proper size?"

"Excuse me?"

"Is his rock big enough for him to get fully out of the water?"

"He needs a rock?"

"Of course he needs a rock, he needs to get out of the water from time to time."

I can imagine the horrified look on my father's face when he learned that, up until that moment, unknown bit of turtle trivia. No one had apparently told my father that Digory would need a rock when he purchased him over a decade ago. In twelve years of ownership, not one visiting friend or family member had ever noticed what was missing in the turtle aquarium up on the shelf of our TV stand. For twelve years, twelve long years, Digory had desperately treaded water, his only respite, anchoring himself to three fake plastic plants where he could rest and only just barely keep his head above water if he craned his neck. He had tried to escape many times from the sadistic family who kept him in hellish torment, but each time he had been recaptured and put back into the nightmare that was his home. Digory wasn't an asshole. We were the assholes.

I'm kind of surprised that even the vet let my father take Digory home with him.  My dad of course was horrified and went out and bought Digory a nice large rock for his aquarium as soon as he left the vet's office.  The moment the rock was placed in the aquarium, Digory climbed out of the water on to it, and did not venture back into the water for at least a month.

# Gooning 101

"Hello."

"Hey. How you doing?"

"Not so bad, how about yourself?"

"Can't complain. Figure it's been a while, probably about time to give you a call. How's everything been?"

"Doing well. Everything good on your end?"

"Pretty well. Been fairly nice the last couple of days. No rain. How have the kids been?"

"Good. Growing like weeds and constantly chattering."

"Good."

"Yeah."

"Been doing anything lately?"

"Not really. You?"

"Not much. I was watching this show on Thomas Edison last night."

"Oh yeah, how was that?"

"Pretty good. Guy was crazy."

"Yeah, I think he hit a certain point where he just kind of lost it."

"I know. What the hell. Guy invents the phonograph and then spends the next six years trying to use it to talk to the dead."

"You know he's responsible for Hollywood being in LA right?"

"Really?"

"Oh yeah, Edison had the patent for the movie camera and wouldn't let anyone else use it without paying exorbitant fees. So all the other movie makers went to Southern California so they could make movies without paying him."

".................."

"Are you there?"

"Yeah, sorry. Thought I heard something. Anyways, everyone goes to Southern California."

"Yeah, they all went to Southern California because it was the farthest place in the US away from Edison and his goons."

"Edison had goons?"

"Oh hell yeah. Rich son of a bitch like that. Guy had to be crawling in goons."

"I guess it makes sense. I can just see a couple of goons shaking down Tesla, you know, telling him that maybe he should think about DC power instead."

"Hey Tesla, maybe you should spend your time lookin into other things. These are some nice boirds youse got, it would be real shame to see something happen to your boirds."

"How the hell does someone even hire goons?"

"I don't know. I can't imagine it's something where you just pick up a couple of big guys off the street."

"What was that?"

"I said, yeah, I can't imagine it's something where you just grab a couple big guys off the street and ask them if they want to start gooning for a moderate fee."

"Sorry, must be a bit of a bad connection. It's probably not something you put in the paper either. Have you ever seen gooning in the want ads?"

"It's probably there. Definitely in all the big business periodicals. They just call it something else to keep it on the down low, like executive assistant or something. You just have to know what you're look for."

"Executive assistant needed. Must be a big burly fellow with a sloping forehead, a love of roughing up others, questionable ethics, and a thick Brooklyn accent."

"Shit, that would be embarrassing if you went in for the wrong thing. Little tiny weedy guy goes in for a so called secretarial job. The interviewer is just sitting there going, hmmm, I don't think you're quite what we're looking for."

"Maybe that's where they get the talky goons."

"The talky goons?"

"Yeah, you know, the little weedy looking goon who does all the talking while the big goons stand behind him and look intimidating. I mean granted, all of my goon knowledge is based off of movies, but he always seems a little out of place."

"Most of the bigger goons probably aren't the best conversationalists."

"Maybe there's some kind of goon hiring service you can call. You know, just get a couple goons for the afternoon."

"That would be a sucky job. You'd have really odd hours and the pay probably ain't great."

"Really? I thought it would be a pretty good job. You really don't do much, just intimidate people every now and again and spend the rest of your time just standing around in someone's outer office. In all those movies there always seems to be some random goons sitting around. Flipping coins, chewing on toothpicks, playing solitaire."

"Hell, there's probably some kind of goon union."

"Goon union?"

"Yeah, all the goons go down to the hiring hall every morning and get sent out to jobs based on their gooning experience. Eddy, we need you to go rough up a green grocer on Elm. Jimmy, go talk to a city councilman at Ms. Sally's tonight, let him know he needs to vote the right way. Louie, go stand around and look intimidating on the corner of Washington and Tenth."

"Lissen up you mugs, lets calls to order this meeting of the International Brotherhood of Goons and Hustlers Local 23."

"Makes sense. If you're a goon you probably have to be a union member."

"Really, no right to work?"

"Who's going to stand up and refuse to join an entire union of goons?"

"Good point......Hey, did you hear something?"

"What?"

"Did you hear something."

"No."

"............"

"Are you there?"

"Yeah. Sorry. Anyways, what happens if the goons go on strike?"

"What the hell would the goons go on strike for?"

"I don't know. Reasonable hours and better quality brass knuckles?"

"I don't imagine a goon strike would last very long."

"No, probably not."

"I really think it would be in your best interest to sign this contract in a hurry. This is a nice office youse got here. It would be a damn shame if someone messed up this nice office."

"Maybe they can get some non-union goons or something?"

"Some goon scabs?"

"Yeah."

"Those would probably be some pretty rough guys. You'd have to be pretty rough to be a goon scab."

"Are you feeling alright?"

"Yeah, I feel fine. Why?"

"You're not breathing hard or anything?"

"No."

"...........
"

"Everything all right?"

"Yeah. It just sounds like your breathing real hard."

"Ummmm."

"Sorry. Probably just my ears playing tricks on me. How does one even get into gooning?"

"Maybe it's something you can take night classes for."

"I don't know. I imagine it's something more like an apprenticeship. You know, you start out just standing in the back and work your way up to being the guy who actually threatens people."

"You probably have to know somebody. That's how most of those union jobs work. It's not just something where you wake up one day and decide to start gooning."

"I don't know. I bet there's lots of people who just start out goon moonlighting."

"Goon moonlighting?"

"Yeah, you know, you just want to make a little extra money. Maybe you just want to try it for a little bit. Your buddy who's been gooning for years asks if you'd be interested in trying it out after a couple of drinks one evening at your local watering hole."

"It would probably be hard to get anyone to hire you if you're just some amateur looking to get started."

"Oh yeah, you probably have to be licensed or something."

"A goon license."

"You've got to let people know somehow that they're hiring a professionally trained goon instead of just some random street tough. People don't want to hire any old riff raff. When you're paying good money you want to know that the person is going to provide the level of service you expect from a professional goon."

"Who the hell would license goons?"

"The National Goon Licensing Board."

"So what, is this like a private organization, or some kind of pseudo government thing."

"It's an NGO."

"I see."

"I know you're listening."

"What?"

"Nothing. Anyways, the board probably sets up all the rules for gooning, you know, skills training, minimum gooning requirements, teaching gooning ethics."

"Gooning ethics?"

"Oh yeah, you have to have gooning ethics, not to mention just learning how to do all the things that goons have to do."

"You mean besides roughing people up and intimidating them."

"Yeah. You know, like sitting around and guarding things. Like the guy who just sits around all day guarding the frozen head of Walt Disney."

"Someones gotta do it."

"My job is to make sure that no Disney executives come down here and lick this head. You'd be surprised how much of a problem that actually is."

"Why the hell would anybody lick Walt Disney's frozen head?"

"I don't know. Good luck or something."

"He'd probably just get bored and start using the head in some weird ventriloquist act."

"See. Now that would definitely be something that would be against the official gooning code of ethics."

"Hmmmm. If there's a goon union and a goon licensing board, I imagine there must be some kind of goon lobby."

"Goon lobby?"

"Yeah, a goon lobby. You know, to make sure Congress doesn't pass any anti-gooning laws. A group to protect the rights of Americans to rough up and intimidate each other."

"It would probably be a pretty successful lobby."

"Youse better vote down this bill Congressman."

"You're really terrible at that accent."

"I know."

"What would happen if the gooning lobby had an opposite opinion on something compared to the people who are hiring goons?"

"What?"

"The goon lobbyist comes into the congressman's office. Youse better vote yes tomorrow. A few minutes later another goon comes in. Youse better vote no. The poor congressman would just be sitting there going, what do I do, I'm so confused."

"They probably have to go the way the goon union tells them to."

"Yeah, that makes sense."

"Of course it makes sense."

"Shhhh."

"What?"

"Do you hear that?"

"Hear what?"

"........."

"Are you okay?"

"I know you're fucking listening."

"Yeah, I'm listening."

"I'm not talking to you. Just hush up for a second."

"Wha...."

"I know you're fucking listening you fucking bastards."

"I....."

"This is a serious infringement of my rights. I'm an American citizen you fascist fucks."

"Look I got to go."

"Yeah, that's probably for the best. Tell the kids hi for me."

"Sure. I'll do that. Bye."

"Bye."

# Nugget

It was all encased in a dream world, everything moving in slow motion and echoes sluggishly rebounding in a semi-liquid atmosphere. The door fell back towards me inch by inch, traveling at half the normal speed until it closed with a resounding click which reverberated as though from some great underwater distance. My synapses, popping at half speed, tried to raise my hand to stop it, but by the time the message was received the door was already closed and locked. None of it really mattered.

My body turned and my legs began wading through the carpet down the hallway which flexed this way and that. My head floated nearly off my shoulders, lifted by the various liquors and alcohols that I had been imbibing since we arrived on Friday. The lights along the ceiling pulsed in time with the slothful beating of my heart. Each movement was a minute, and each minute was forever. Time no longer had any meaning. I had escaped its grasp at last, and I was free to go wherever I wanted. No fears, no problems, no anxieties. I stopped to look at a painting on the wall, flowers and fruit, and started laughing hysterically, the sound, let loose, bounding down the corridor.

The world sped back up to normal when the scream split the air. The dream world disappeared and I found myself sprawled on the thirty year old design of golds and browns which made up the carpet on top of a tipped over maid's cart. Little bottles of shampoo, lotion, mouthwash, and conditioner skittered across the floor. A short Hispanic woman in a gray dress and flats was already halfway down the hall, making the turn into the alcove and door marked for staff only. I was completely naked.

It's a strange thing to be a sleepwalker. To fall asleep in one place and to wake up in another. It's disorienting to say the least. Add the cloudiness of a two day bender in a city known for sin and vice and it can be downright frightening. Imagine for yourself, one moment you're drifting off to sleep cuddled against the warm soft flesh of some woman you met at the roulette table, in the gentle sway of post-coital drunken bliss, and the next you're sprawled nude in the hallway with the sounds of a maid screaming like a banshee receding into the distance.

All feelings of bliss and contentment disappeared in just an instant. The world became suddenly over focused and my overwatered mind desperately tried to make sense of, and plan an appropriate response to, the situation. Five doors down, an old man with a white mustache peaked out, his eyes met mine, grew wide, then retreated back into his sanctuary. Shit. This was not good. This was not ideal. This was very bad. Where the hell was I?

Memories bubbled up in my brain, little snippets of recollections. Laughing at unheard jokes, a hand reaching forward to touch mine, watching a zipliner move under the televised dome of old town Vegas, fruity drinks served by shivering bikini clad women, kissing in a dark corner by the slots, a smiling redhead leading me by the hand back to her room. Room, that's it. I needed to find her room. Keys, wallet, watch, phone, clothes, everything, everything was in that room. I looked up and down the hallway. Rows of identical white doors separated by gold and cream striped walls. Everything looked the same.

I started jogging back the way I had come, covering myself with one hand. Room 1247, 1246, 1245. Which one was the right one? I gazed at each matching door imploringly, hoping for some glimmer of recognition. My brain began to tumble into panic, I didn't have much time, even in Vegas a random naked man can only run through the hallways for so long. Perhaps if I went back to the elevator, maybe if I retraced my steps my subconscious would remember. Maybe....wait.....room 1233. That seemed familiar. I felt drawn to 1233, something niggling at the back of my mind. Was this the right room? I stood at the door unsure what to do. What if it was the wrong room?

Victory goes to those who take the risk. I raised my arm and gave the door a few loud knocks. No answer. I knocked harder. No answer. A sense of panic began to set in. I raised my fist back and pounded hard enough to make the door shake. Still nothing. I was about to redouble my efforts when I felt a presence behind me. The feeling that somebody was watching. I turned slowly, my genitals still protectively cupped, and looked at two security guards standing just five feet away, watching me. They were both big and solid, with buzz cut hair and heavy muscles just starting to go to fat.

"What the hell do you think you're doing?" growled the one on the right.

I tried a disarming smile, but their faces remained stony, and I felt it die before it was even fully born. My brain, still sluggish, was a few seconds behind the rest of the world.

The one on the right growled again. "Excuse me, what the hell do you think you're doing?"

"My stuff is in this room."

"I very much doubt that."

The seconds ticked by as my brain came up with a proper response. "Why do you doubt that?"

"Because that rooms empty, there's no one currently staying in it."

I tried to focus on the man's words, keep my eyes focused on his mouth to help me better discern what he was saying, but I could feel them constantly skittering away to look down the hall behind him or at the curling cord that snaked its way from his ear into his collar. My brain struggled to find an appropriate response to the sudden change in reality.

The bored looks of the security guards began to change to impatience. The one on the left spoke up, with a voice even gravellier than the one on the right. "Sir, are you staying at this hotel?"

"No." That was an easy one, a question without complications.

"Then what are you doing here?"

"A woman brought me here." My face contorted into an odd combination of pleased with myself smile and flushed embarrassment. The security guards' expressions didn't change. "I was sleepwalking and the door shut behind me. I don't know which is the right one."

The security guard on the left snickered a little bit. His partner just sneered, his eyes brushing over me with a disinterest that made me somehow feel more uncomfortable with my nudity. The one on the left seemed the nicer of the two so I concentrated on him. His lips were still slightly curled up and his voice sounded less harsh in my ears.

"Shit, that's a new one. Okay, just tell us this gals name and we'll escort you to her room to make sure your story checks out."

Shit. Name, what the hell was her name? A thousand possibilities swam through my head in an instant. None seemed right. What was her name? Did we even exchange names?

What kind of hedonistic place was this where two people could do those kind of things to each other and not even know the proper word to call one another? She had asked me to call her something earlier in the night, soon after we got to her room, but I was pretty damned sure that word was not her name.

The seconds ticked into a minute and the silence became deafening. The friendly face of the security guard on the left became a frown. In contrast, the face of the security guard on the right twisted into a small smile, though his eyes remained cold. Here was a man who obviously enjoyed his work. The one on the left gave a little sigh.

"I'm afraid we're going to have to escort you off the premises sir."

The two men began to advance and I felt very small and scared. "Wait....wait," I stammered, "you can't throw me out on the street like this. For god sakes, I'm completely naked."

The two men stopped and looked at each other for a moment. Their eyes locked in silent debate and finally the one on the right gave a little groan before turning and stalking back up the hallway. The other security guard and I stood staring at each other, neither having anything to say, until his partner came back up the hallway and handed me a white terrycloth robe and a pair of hotel slippers. They waited patiently while I donned my new finery and then pushed me firmly towards the elevator.

Down the elevator, out a long hallway with a view of the pool, past a lobby with marble counters and pillars, through the always crowded casino, and out the Fremont Street entrance of the Golden Nugget casino. With me safely deposited on the sidewalk, out of their jurisdiction, the two security guards turned to head back inside.

"Wait," I called at their backs. "Could you please tell me what time it is?"

The friendlier one turned and checked his watch but did not stop walking. "Four thirty in the afternoon," he said as he disappeared inside.

Shit. How could it already be four thirty in the afternoon? How late, or I guess early, did I go to bed last night? It was a problem. Time doesn't exist in Vegas, but that rule doesn't apply to the rest of the world. Leo, Dean, Paul, and myself. We all had to be at work on Monday morning. That was the one stipulation when we agreed to the trip. The one rule. It was just a short getaway. A guy's weekend to help me forget the recently signed divorce papers. A quick burst of excitement before going back to the drudge of the world.

I started running down Fremont Street. Pushing my way past afternoon drunks gawking at the overhead flashing light of the giant television screen. Maneuvering around families grinning at the statue men painted gold and silver. Bobbing and weaving to avoid the man pretending he didn't notice his wife's angry looks as he stared at the Vegas dancers. The sun seemed overly bright and hurt my eyes. My head began to pound with every step and I felt dizzy. My Golden Nugget slippers came off and disappeared behind me. I kept running. Past the Four Queens, past the Fremont, past The D, past the Brass Lounge, and past Hennessey's. I ran out of the pedestrian area, onto the street, and didn't stop until I was in the garish black and white lobby of the El Cortez.

I paused in the doorway to catch my breath, bent over, hands on my knees. An old man sitting in a chair in the corner looked up from his newspaper, gave me an uninterested look, and then returned to the headlines. The two of us were alone. I walked to the front desk, my bare feet cold on the black and white tile, and rang the bell. The sound echoed through the lobby. A stuffy little man with a thin mustache and perfectly primped hair walked in from the back. He was impeccably dressed in a suit and tie, though the hotel did not require him to be. His eyes

94

quickly darted up and down, taking me all in. The man smiled at me with slightly crooked teeth like he was my oldest friend in the world.

The little man's voice had a slight lisp to it and his pauses were longer than they needed to be. "Mr. Johnson…, how good to see you again. It looks like you've had an… interesting day."

I nodded back. "You could say that. Are my friends still here?"

The little man's smile changed to a look of sadness and distress. "No, I'm sorry…, Misters Peskin, Leary, and Schlesinger left about an hour ago."

"Shit." I didn't mean to curse but the word just slipped out. I could see my three friends crowded into Leo's little Volvo, speeding up Highway 58 on the eight hour drive back to Sacramento.

The little man smiled warmly. "Yes…, they were very flustered that you weren't here and they felt… oh so terrible about leaving. Oh…, and they also left you this."

The little man rummaged under the counter and produced a white envelope which he handed to me with great flourish. I tore it open and pulled out its contents, just a note and a baggage claim ticket. The note said:

> Dave,
> Where the fuck are you? We've tried your phone several times and nobody answers. We've been waiting for six hours and we can't wait any longer. Both Paul and I have to get up at five in the morning tomorrow. Sorry to leave you behind. We put your luggage in storage here at the hotel.
>
> Dean

I looked at the letter in my hand and felt like cursing again. Dean would have wanted to wait as long as possible. Leo and Paul were a little more libertarian about such things. I could see Leo clenching his jaw and kneading his fist like he does when he's angry but doesn't want to show it. I couldn't really blame them for leaving. I would have done the same thing in their position. They weren't the only ones who had a Monday work day they couldn't afford to miss. My friends had only been gone an hour. If I had my phone, I could give them a call and they'd probably come back. But my phone was locked in some unknown hotel room at the Golden Nugget, and I knew none of my friend's phone numbers by heart.

I looked up at the smiling little man who looked as though he didn't have a trouble in the world. I traded in the luggage ticket for my small blue duffle bag. At least I had a change of clothes.

"Would it be alright if I used your bathroom?"

"Of course…, it's just right over there."

I opened my duffel bag in the bathroom, which had the same black and white decor as the lobby. Pickings were slim. It was a weekend trip and I had packed accordingly. Events earlier in the weekend had cut down my options further. A Hawaiian shirt, a pair of Bermuda shorts, and flip flops. Attire for the Jimmy Buffett concert we attended Friday night. A tightly wrapped garbage bag containing a button down shirt and a pair of blue jeans. Both covered in vomit courtesy of a friendly but overly inebriated stranger we ran into on Fremont Street on Saturday afternoon. My toiletries kit was missing.

I went into a stall and wisely chose the Hawaiian shirt and Bermuda shorts. I shoved the bathrobe into my duffel bag. There was no reason to throw out a perfectly good bathrobe. Exiting the stall, the mirror over the sinks gave me the first good look at myself since I had woken up. My hair was mussed and badly tangled. My eyes were bloodshot, the skin under them dark and puffy. My facial hair was cut into a somewhat bedraggled looking fu manchu, something Paul had thought would be hilarious for the Jimmy Buffett concert. I looked in essence, like crap.

With the clothing issue solved I felt a bit better, and took stock of my situation. It was not good. I was still stranded in Vegas with no money, no phone, and no way home. A more intensive search of my duffle bag did not turn up many solutions. Eighty-seven cents in loose change, a half used pack of gum, an unopened box of condoms, an old candy bar wrapper, four dollars worth of chips from the Four Queens, and a ball gag that Leo had sneaked into my bag as a joke. At the very least I had the makings of becoming a so-so prostitute, but I really hoped it wouldn't come down to that.

There was one thing I hadn't checked yet. The tightly wrapped garbage bag containing my puke covered clothes sat at the bottom of the duffle bag. Desperate times called for desperate measures. I took a few deep breaths, stopped breathing, and unrolled the garbage bag. The stench was overwhelming. It wafted upward like a cloud of bad memories. I had tried to hand wash the clothes a bit in the sink after the incident, but it had obviously not been enough. I felt my stomach attempting to heave itself upwards, but I forced it back down and did a thorough search of my sodden clothes.

My hands were clumsy in my haste. Everything was still damp. The pants had little to offer, just an after dinner mint and another dollar casino chip, this one from the Golden Gate. The shirt though, the shirt contained the answer to my salvation and made the suffering worth it. A small flat square in the front pocket, a little piece of plastic salvation. God only knows what events led it to be in my shirt pocket instead of my wallet. I took it out and felt my eyes begin to grow moist with relief, though most likely it was just the smell. My credit card shown like a bright beacon in the stark light of the bathroom.

I hastily rolled my soiled clothes back up in the garbage sack and shoved them back into my bag. I washed both my hands and the credit card thoroughly. Things would have to be done right. It was the credit card that had been the main financier of the trip. It had paid for the hotel room, gas, drinks, and a couple of meals. It didn't have a high limit. There probably wasn't that much left on it. Definitely not enough for an airline ticket. But most likely enough for at least a rental car.

I exited the bathroom and the little man behind the counter lifted his head from his computer screen and smiled at me again. "Oh, don't you just look... delicious."

I tried to smile back to be polite. "Thanks. Do you know of any really cheap car rental places nearby?"

"On a bit of a budget... are we?"

"Yeah, you could say that."

The little man made a great show of thinking deeply. "Well....probably your best bet would be Lucky Car Rentals. It's down at the Main Street Station Casino. You just walk out that little old door... and take a right... and after one block take a left down Stewart. You can't miss it."

"Thanks."

As I walked out the door I could hear the little man yell behind me. "No problem at all. Hope you come back to Vegas soon." I'm glad my back was turned. It hid the grimace on my face at the thought of coming back.

Outside it was still hot as hell, with an unbearably bright sun hanging overhead and not a single cloud to provide relief. I walked up the street, my duffle bag thrown over my shoulder, my flip flops popping with every step. The damn city was like an oven. I could feel sweat trickling down my back and inundating the armpits of my shirt. I felt like I was under the interrogation light in an old cop movie. Everything about the situation was uncomfortable.

Up one block and take a left down Stewart. I was only two blocks from the tourist drag that was Fremont Street, but it felt like I was in an entirely different city. Small businesses and parking garages lined the avenue. The people who wandered about looked like locals, but even their numbers were limited. It felt like I was in a small desert town in Arizona or New Mexico. Some out of the way place that nobody ever went to unless they had to.

I saw a convenience store on my right. My mouth suddenly felt very dry and parched. remembered that I hadn't had anything to eat or drink since I'd woken up. I crossed the street and walked across the empty parking lot. Two teenagers sat outside next to the newspaper box. Both had stringy greasy hair and dirty faces. Their clothes were ripped and patched and so filthy they appeared brown with only occasional swaths of vivid brightness to show their former color. They watched me walk up. I ignored them.

The door beeped as I walked in and a refreshing blast of cold air slammed into me. The man behind the counter was a big intimidating guy who looked like he belonged on the road with the Hell's Angels, or maybe one of the lesser known gangs like the Mongols. He looked up at me and then went back to reading the classifieds. I used the spare change from my duffel bag to buy a generic pop, something called Alpine Mist, and headed back outside.

I paused and cracked open the can and took a deep drink. It tasted terrible, like carbonated pool water with sugar added. I looked around me and met the eye of one of the hoodlums sitting next to the newspaper box.

"Hey man," his voice was petulant and grated in my ears, "give us some money."

I don't know what came over me. Normally I'm fairly even-keeled, pretty good at letting things just slide off of me. A regular I'm rubber you're glue kind of guy. Maybe it was the fact that I was tired, dehydrated, and still half-drunk. Maybe it was the heat or the headache from the overly bright sun. Whatever it was, I suddenly found myself past my breaking point.

My voice boomed across the parking lot. "Fuck off, you little worthless piece of fucking shit!"

My middle finger rose in a salute, and I turned and walked away, taking another drink from the can in my hand. I was halfway across the parking lot when I heard the footsteps coming. I was half turned around when the fist hit the back of my head and I went sprawling. The can of pseudo-soda flew from my hand, neon yellow fluid pouring across the asphalt. I curled into a tight little ball and did my best to protect my head as the two kids punched and kicked me. It couldn't have lasted more than thirty seconds.

"Hey," yelled a loud deep voice, "get the fuck out of here, I've called the police!"

The two kids scattered, one getting in a last kick to my back before he fled. I uncurled and looked up in time to see the convenience store worker shaking his head and walking back inside. Cursing, I sat on the ground for a bit and spat a wad of blood and snot onto the pavement. I sat there for a bit, but finally seeing that nobody was going to come out and help me I got up and continued walking down the street towards the Main Street Casino.

It took about ten minutes to walk the remaining five blocks. I felt bruised and a little shaken, but nothing too serious. I breathed a sigh of relief when I walked into the front office of the Lucky Car Rental, which the sign outside bragged was the luckiest car rental place in Vegas. I didn't really know what that was supposed to mean, but I didn't feel like now was the time to be too choosy. The woman behind the front desk was a gaunt shrewish woman, nothing but sharp angles and deep lines covered in thick makeup. She looked up as I walked in and I saw her eyes grow wide. A customer service smile dying before it even began.

"Hi, I'm here to rent a car."

Her eyes worked their way up and down and her posture became stiff and guarded. "I'm sorry sir, we don't have any available cars to rent." Her tone was cold and unyielding.

I looked through the window behind her at the interior of a garage full of shiny freshly waxed cars sitting in neat little rows. I looked back down at her unblinking gaze. I felt like I was involved in a staring contest.

"Really, you have no cars available to rent at all?"

"That's what I said. I don't think I stuttered."

My fists began to clench involuntarily. I could feel anger start to well up in me. It churned from the inside out and I could sense that I was going to blow at any second. She obviously saw it too. Her hand moved down and picked up the receiver of the telephone. The fingers of her other hovered over the keypad. Her eyes never left mine, they seemed to be daring me to challenge her authority and control of the situation. I let out a defeated sigh and turned to walk out.

As I walked back towards the exit, I saw my reflection in the glass door. Shit, no wonder she was looking at me that way. I looked even more like crap than I had in the hotel bathroom mirror. My entire front and right side were covered in dirt, my Hawaiian shirt was ripped and several of the buttons were missing, and my face and front were covered in blood. I stopped and put a hand to my face, but a cleared throat behind me reminded me it was time to move on. I pushed open the door and walked out.

A little reordering was definitely needed before I made another attempt. I snuck through the side entrance into the casino and found the nearest bathroom where I washed the dirt and blood off of my face and arms. I then found a gift shop and bought the cheapest hat and shirt I could find. The hat had an oversized brim and was neon yellow with Vegas spelled across the front in big red letters. The shirt had a giant roaring lion head covering the entire front. I paid for both items with my credit card, hoping that the small amount wouldn't put me too close to the limit to rent a car to get home.

Looking once again close to a proper citizen, I walked down the street to the next casino on the row, the Plaza Hotel and Casino, hoping to find another car rental place. I didn't dare go back to Lucky. My luck was with me. The Plaza had a major chain rental car place in it. This one had another shrewish gaunt woman behind the front desk who could have been the sister of the woman at the Lucky Car Rental. However, this one didn't put away her fake smile when I walked in."

"Hello. How can I help you?"

"I need to rent a car please. Something cheap that I can drop off in Sacramento tomorrow."

"Oh of course sir." She tapped away on her computer, idly chewing on a piece of gum. "Will you be wanting the insurance?"

"No."

She typed away again and then turned back to me. "Okay, one economy sized car with drop off at our branch in Sacramento and no insurance, with taxes and fees that comes out to sixty-five dollars and twenty-eight cents."

"Perfect."

"Okay, now you just give me a credit card and a driver's license and we can get you all set up."

Shit.

"I don't have my driver's license."

"Sir, you can't rent a car if you don't have a driver's license."

"No, I have one, I just don't have it with me."

"Sir, I'm going to need a valid driver's license before I can rent you this car."

All of the energy seemed to collapse out of me. I felt my knees grow weak and I had to put my hand on her desk to keep from falling down. I tried to talk several times, but nothing came out of my mouth. She looked at me inquiringly and suddenly the entire story of my day burst forth in a flurry of words and explanations. All of my pride, all of my self-respect, went out the window as I related my woes to her. I never cried or anything like that, but I made it fairly obvious that I was coming close to doing so.

For her part, the woman never once dropped her fake smile. She listened attentively and even made sympathetic noises at appropriate parts of my story. When I reached the end she reached across the desk and put her hand with its brightly painted fingernails on mine and said, "you poor dear, that just all sounds so terrible."

I tried a weak smile in thanks. "So you're going to rent me a car?"

"God no, they'd have my ass canned before you even left the office. You can't get a car without a valid driver's license."

I felt all hope slowly dissipate from my being. I was trapped and I was never going to get out of here. "What am I suppose to do?"

The woman's face screwed into a look of concentration. "Well, you could always try the bus, the station is just a few blocks up the street."

I left the car rental office and walked back up the street to the bus station. It was a squat dingy building with big silvery busses lined up outside. The interior was dirty with bad lighting and well worn wooden benches holding people who all looked as tired and worn out as I felt. A short frog looking man sat behind glass along one wall, his unshaven jaw clenched around an unlit cigar. I waited in line until the two people ahead of me finished their inquiries and purchases and stepped up to the window.

"What can I do for you?" The man's voice even sounded a bit like a frog.

"I'd like a bus ticket to Sacramento please."

The man looked over a schedule table on the wall and looked back at me. "Next bus leaves for Sacramento at 8 AM tomorrow morning."

I felt my heart drop once again. "There's nothing else sooner?" My voice sounded plaintive and pathetic.

The man turned and looked over his tables again, running his finger down columns and across rows. "Shit, my bad. There's an overnighter to Sacramento that leaves tonight at 8 PM."

I stared at the frog on the other side of the glass, imagining my hands around his throat.

"You want a ticket for that one?"

"Yeah."

"That will be ninety-two dollars." I handed my credit card through the hole in the window and he took it and turned it around in his hands, examining it with great care.

"Can I see some identification?"

"I lost my identification."

"Hmmm…." The froggish man looked at my credit card and chewed on his cigar. He looked up at me and then back at the card. I found myself silently praying in my head to a multitude of heavenly deities to help me. Finally he pushed a pen and sheet of paper through the hole in the window. "Sign your signature five times on this piece of paper."

I complied with his demand and pushed the pen and paper back through the hole. He picked up the paper and held it and the credit card close to his eyes. He squinted at one and then the other. Back and forth for a full minute.

"What the hell, close enough for me."

I tried to keep an elated smile from erupting across my face. The little froggy man printed the ticket and pushed it, my credit card, and a receipt through the hole to me. I signed the receipt and pushed it back, picked up my credit card and ticket, holding both very tightly, and found myself a spot on the wooden bench to wait. I had only been up for a little more than an hour, but the moment my butt hit that bench I felt more tired than I'd ever felt before. I felt like I hadn't slept a single hour for the entire weekend. My head nodded onto my chest, and the world all just seemed to drift away.

I'm lucky I didn't miss the bus. A kindly old lady woke me up when it was time to board. A group of us derelicts and ne'er-do-wells were herded onto the great silvery beast and I found myself seated next to the same kindly old lady. By the time the bus lurched into motion she was already asleep with her head on my shoulder. Her breath smelled like old milk and asparagus.

As the bus left the city I looked out the window at the setting sun. It was only then that I realized that I probably should have tried to leave some kind of message at the Golden Nugget for the poor girl who probably woke up sometime that afternoon completely alone with a room full of abandoned menswear. I don't know how I could have done it without a name or room number, but I could have tried. At the very least I should have gone back to check the Golden Nugget's lost and found for my possessions.

Oh well. Credit cards, drivers license, cell phone, house keys, they can all get replaced. None of the damage was permanent. It was just inconvenient. Nothing really mattered now. Not the misadventure in Vegas, not the foul breath of the old woman drooling on my shoulder, not the fact that my friends left me behind, not the recently signed divorce papers. Not one bit of it mattered. I was finally heading home.

# Melancholy

It's a frightening thing. At times I sit and imagine stories. Stories of horror, stories of tragedy. My father died when I was just a boy. I was adopted by a family that never loved me. The accident took the majority of my family away from me. I had to fight. Fight for everything I had. They are all pieces of fiction. The struggles I have faced in my life seem so small, so unimportant compared to the struggles of so many people in the world. It's strange to imagine such things. Even yearn for them at times. Something, just something. Something to give reason to the ways that I feel inside. That sense of melancholy that has followed me from the time I was a very small child. That sense of not belonging. That sense of being apart.

The joys of those around me have always seemed to escape me. I look at them with jealousy and hate myself for feeling such things. I have been given a loving family. I have been given intelligence. I have been given charm when I have the confidence to use it. I have been given so much, so many things. I wouldn't give away any of these things, but it never seems like enough. There has always been a yearning, a yearning for something that I cannot see nor really understand. It's been a part of me for as long as I can remember. Contentment, the word is contentment. In my mind I don't think I'll ever truly have it, not for long at any rate. The short moments in my life made just a taste, just enough to keep me going forward. I try my best to help others when I can, help others to have what I cannot, and weep privately and secretly for the lead actor in my own tragedy.

It is not a good thing to feel too sorry for yourself. When you feel too sorry for yourself you begin making excuses and letting yourself go down a path of no return. You become selfish. You begin to see those around you as nothing but things. We forget to care. I try to avoid going down such a path as much as possible, but I would be lying if I claimed I never failed.

# An E-Mail

Maybe it's a form of madness, or maybe a form of obsession. It's a scary thought, but I don't know. I don't have enough to disprove it. Maybe I could if I asked someone else's opinion, but I've never been one to do that. I can talk for hours about someone else's problems. I can provide a listening ear and a bit of advice when needed. I can act as someone else's barometer. But when it comes to myself I find it difficult to open up I find it difficult to let the plea for help pass through my lips. It's a strange thing, that I can be a rock for people when needed, but have my own foundations be so crumbly.

I don't do well with waiting. I'm not good at sitting still and doing nothing. The email has been sent, and now I'm doing busy work around the house, trying to keep myself occupied. I sweep the floor, my motions quick and hard, dust bunnies skitter across the room, thrown forward by the ferocity of my movements. My stomach is in knots, my back is tense and tight to the point that it hurts. I have trouble concentrating. The carefully chosen words of the email flash through my mind again and again.

Helen,

I'm sorry for Friday night. You're right that I can
never know how you feel inside. You are a
wonderful person and your anxiety is such a small
part of who you are. I wish you could talk about
it again, like you used to. I wish you would talk
so I could just listen, and learn, like I should have
when you trusted me enough to talk about it.

I've made it no secret that given a chance I would
date you again in a second, I understand that this
won't happen, but it doesn't matter. I will always
care about you. You are an amazing person in so
many ways. My friendship is freely given for as
long as you want it, no matter what.

I'll see you Friday at Molly's birthday. I promise
not to talk about this kind of stuff. I'm always
willing to listen, opinions only given upon
request.

Did I choose the right words? Did I convey the right
tone? Did I say enough? I know I didn't say enough. I know I
didn't say nearly enough. I had wanted to convey all that I
knew. I wanted to tell her all the things that I had in my mind. It
was too much, just too much. It would be overwhelming. I
don't want to overwhelm her. I don't want to hurt her. So I hold
back. I hold back and don't say many of the things I should.
What about how she is hurting herself the more she avoids it?
What about the things that happened with Molly last weekend?
So many things that I know, so many things that are pertinent
and germane. So many things left unsaid.

Quotes and arguments flow through my head. Desperate plans and stirring speeches that go to the heart of her soul and break through the walls she has built. They flow through my head like water. Things I need to say, but will never have the guts to say. The strident, demanding, and fervent anger of a man who knows that the things that he preaches are true. So long in the wilderness. So long alone. I am not the only one who sees it. I am not the only one who knows. It is not all just in my head. It is not all just the ramblings of a crazed mind.

My mind is desperate for anything to think about. It dredges up wrongs and arguments of the past. It goes through and over every single thing that we have ever said to each other. It identifies the wrongs she has done to me. It remembers every misstep I took. It opens old debates and fights them once again. One way arguments that still end without a winner. I try to override it. I try to remember happy memories, but my mind argues that there are none. My life is one of misery and sadness, and happiness was just an imagined fantasy. There is so much I want to forget. I have accomplished so much, but I have failed to even put a dent in the walls that surround her. It has been nearly a year since I took up the fight. I know so much, but all my knowledge is useless. All that I have done has proven pointless and fruitless. Empty eyes. How can I bring myself to face the empty eyes again?

I am not good at waiting. I only sent the email yesterday evening. I hold myself back from checking my inbox constantly, or getting onto Facebook to check to see if her profile has been updated. I know these are pointless and unhealthy things to do. I do it because it gives me just a small sense of actively doing something. Work is the worst. The internet is at my fingers at all times. I always get my work done too quickly and have too much free time to let my mind wander. Energy courses through my body, demanding action. Demanding that I do something right now to solve the problem. The email has been sent. She will reply if she wants to. I know I must be patient, I know I must wait, these are the logical things to do. But my body does not want logic, my body is demanding I do something right now. I go for a run instead, hoping that I can wear my body down to the point where it feels nothing.

Shoes hit the street one after another, pushing my body forward. I push myself harder and harder. My breath becomes ragged. I'm running as fast as I can, trying to outdistance my thoughts, trying to outrun the truth. Lies. There are lies in the email I sent. I know that I won't be able to leave it behind. I know that I won't be able to ignore the things I see, or not say the things I know. I'm trapped. There are so many things that I know I have to say, but if I do then all will be lost. My ship of hope has foundered, and the only way to complete my mission is to sink it to the bottom. This is but a stop gap. I know I won't be able to last much longer. I know I am in my last desperate efforts. I know I am failing. I am failing in that she is not understanding. I am failing in that I am not brave enough or strong enough to destroy everything I have with her to try and save her.

Faster and faster. My lungs burn and my sides ache. Into the park, under the shade of the trees, a few leaves just starting to show the color of early fall. I want so desperately to stay a part of her life. I want so desperately to not rock the boat, to bail out the water and put things on the mend, but I cannot. I know that I cannot watch and say nothing. I know it is only a matter of time before I am overcome. Before my boat drifts down underneath the waves. I will stand on the prow and salute the world, a martyr that will not be remembered or appreciated. I'm not going to be able to last much longer. I don't have much left in me. I know the end is coming near. I know that soon I'm going to have to admit that I have failed.

I can't go any further. My legs grow rubbery and I feel them collapse beneath me. My body falls as though in slow motion, down into the soft grass, wet from recent rains. There is nothing I can do. There is nothing I can do. I am going to fail. I have failed her. I have failed myself. This is ruining my life. I knew it would be this way. I knew I could not succeed. Tears stream from my eyes and I beat the ground with my fist in useless frustration. I can't abandon her to her anxiety, but I can't even get her to admit that the anxiety exists.

Waiting is always easier after a few days. All of the energy and hope that has gone into the attempt has largely dissipated by that time. My primal mind has largely gotten the idea that nothing terrible will happen immediately, so it ratchets down from full red alert to yellow alert. No need to panic right now, but stay at battle stations. The need to do something immediately has weakened, it only rears its head occasionally, usually when I have nothing else to occupy my mind. Where once I felt my body was overflowing with energy, now I just feel a dull steady tension. My shoulders and back ache. There is a knot just below my lowest right rib. My stomach hurts. I'm shitting more than normal. I feel tired, drained, a warrior back from combat with a foe that I cannot defeat.

The logical mind has had a chance to review the possibility of failure and come to terms with what that means. It has started making plans on what will happen if no answering email ever comes back. It has started thinking about a future where I have failed. What will I do? Where will I direct my energies? Just because the mind can come to grips with something doesn't mean it's still not sad and depressing. A dull ache in my soul matches the dull ache of my body. At times I catch myself looking out my window at work, just watching the world float by and not really feeling anything.

I am not good at waiting. For a moment I begin to open my email on my computer. I quickly close it again. I could easily make up an excuse for myself, some reason why I need to check my email. But I know that the excuse would be a lie. I know why I would be doing it. It's a trap that I cannot allow myself to fall into. It doesn't take much to throw yourself off of the cliff. To find yourself checking your email every hour, looking through Facebook posts, reading old messages. Analyzing and interpreting everything in a hope of understanding something that I cannot understand.

She would call it an obsession. I think of it more as a fear of the unknown. Her interpretation is probably the more accurate. A fevered mind can create truths where there are none. A fevered mind can change the world to better match the world which it hopes for. I am smart enough to realize these things, to know that I am just as susceptible as anyone else. But I am not smart enough to keep myself from getting too close to the edge. I must keep myself from falling. The closer I stay the more likely I am to slip.

Self-reflection can be a dangerous thing for the waiting mind. It can see all of its mistakes. It can view everything it has done and wonder if perhaps all of the good intentions in the world have led you too far down the rabbit hole. It makes you wonder if you have crossed the line of trying to help and trying to be understood to the point of derangement and lunacy. It would be good to have somebody to talk to about these things. Somebody with which I could share everything. But it's too late, I have been silent too long. The story is now too lengthy to tell. Too many mistakes. Too many missteps. Too many times of trying and failing. The length is only an excuse not to talk to anybody. In truth, I'm afraid that if I do they will point out that I've taken it too far, that I've gone insane.

The work day ends just as the work days before it. I flee my office to spend the evening running with the hash. When I'm around people I'm safe. When I'm around people it is easy to avoid the constant pressure to do something immediately. People provide a distraction and a refuge. It's the times that I'm alone that I'm afraid. With no one else around my only company is my own thoughts, my own doubts, my own worry that I'm losing control of myself. I can only lie to myself so much. I can only convince myself that I can handle the pressure for so long. Sleep is a welcome release from my mental toils. If only I could sleep for as long as it takes. How wonderful that would be.

# Lugnut

He should have listened to his mother. The big red dog sits on its haunches, looking at the boy sitting on the floor next to him directly in the eye. It is a steady, unblinking gaze. Two circular black islands in two matching golden seas. The boy's hand moves slowly and rhythmically through the dogs long red coat from the top of the dog's head to the middle of its back. The boy's fingers disappear into the fur with each stroke, the knuckles brushing against the stiff hairs of the outer coat, while the fingertips feel the softness of the inner layer.

The dog's body is ramrod straight, every muscle resting between tautness and relaxation. A military officer standing at ease, but ready to spring to attention at any moment. The big red tail sits on the ground behind the dog, limp and unmoving. No happy wag, no joyous shake, no sign of appreciation for the boy's constant efforts. Up and down, up and down, up and down. The same motion repeatedly, the same scene again and again.

"Stay away from Lugnut, he isn't good with kids."

The warning echoes in the boy's ears. A firm reminder given every time they've made the hour long car trip to visit his grandmother. It is part of the constant litany of dos and don'ts which dictate the laws of his childhood.

"Lugnut isn't like the dogs at home. Lugnut doesn't spend a lot of time around kids. Don't try to play with Lugnut."

The boy had doubted his mother's words. His seven year old brain had done the calculation and decided that she didn't know what she was talking about. Lugnut wasn't a bad dog, he was just misunderstood, that's all. Given a chance, Lugnut could be treated just like any other dog. Uncle Bill had owned Lugnut for years. Why wouldn't he be used to having kids around?

Yes, Uncle Bill was a bachelor whose house was conspicuously absent of children. Yes, Lugnut was a cow dog who spent most of his life walking behind horses up narrow trails and chasing cattle through forest covered hills. Yes, Lugnut undoubtedly lacked some of the finer social graces and patience that were required when dealing with the sixty pound miniature people that sometimes appeared in his life. But these things just suggested the need for a little tact, not outright ostracization.

The boy had been around dogs his entire life. Some of his earliest memories involved dogs. When the boy thought of himself, he thought of a boy who knew dogs. He knew their behaviors and their signals. He knew the signs that showed what a dog was feeling. Whether it was happy, bored, afraid, or angry. He knew to go slow so that the dog did not get startled. He knew to be careful around a strange dog. But Lugnut was not a strange dog. Lugnut was Uncle Bill's dog. He was pretty much a member of the family.

This trip was going to be different. As the car had carried him and his brothers towards their grandmother's house, and his mother gave the familiar warning, the boy had decided that he was going to prove his mother wrong in her assertions over the personality qualities of Lugnut. This was going to be the trip where his mother, with all her rules and regulations, would have to admit that she was wrong about something. This time she would have to recognize that she didn't know everything and that the boy was not a little kid anymore.

The boy's chance had come shortly after lunch. The adults all sat in the living room, relaxing after the meal and discussing various adult topics and pleasantries. A background drone of catching up on the latest happenings and doings of various other adults and their progeny. His brothers sat on the floor, playing with plastic horses and metal matchbox cars, lost in worlds of adventure within the theaters of their own heads.

The boy put down the metal miniature corvette he was playing with, stood up, and walked down the hall as though he was going to the bathroom. No one in the room looked up to watch him go. The adults were all engrossed in a story about some neighbor. The boy's brothers were reaching the climaxes of their individual internal monologues. The boy walked down the hall, but he did not go to the bathroom. When he was sure no one was looking, the boy turned the corner and went into the kitchen instead.

The big red dog lays in the corner on an old rug next to the door to the outside, waiting for the alpha to get done and head back out to work. His body rose and fell as though he was sleeping, rhythmically in a steady cadence in time with the quiet sound of in rushing and out rushing air from the big dog's nose. With the boy's first step into the kitchen the golden eyes pulled open and the red head raised up from between the big front paws. The dog stared at the boy and the boy stared back. The dog's eyes appraised the miniature person who had entered the room and found nothing of interest. The big head lay back between the large paws, but the eyes did not droop back close. They stayed open, watching.

The boy walked further into the kitchen. The only sounds were his feet upon the floor, the steady movement of air through the dog's stuffed up nose, and the hum of the refrigerator.

"Hey Lugnut, how are you doing today?"

The dog gave no sign that he had heard the question. The boy took a few more steps, and then stopped. He lowered himself to the floor into a cross legged position in the center of the room. The linoleum felt cool beneath him. The golden eyes of the dog followed his every movement with an air of boredom and disinterest. The boy stared back and studied the contours of the eighty pound pile of fur before him. The boy slowed his breathing until it moved in synchronization with that of the dog's. The two remained still, appraising the situation.

One minute, two minutes, three minutes. Time passed with no action by either party. The boy sat and watched the dog. Letting the dog get used to his presence. Letting the dog understand that the boy was not a threat in anyway. The dog laid in the corner and watched the boy. The boy got a sense that the dog was not really all that interested in him, that he only watched him because he was the newest item in the room and therefore slightly more interesting than the other things already in the dog's field of vision. The boy cleared his throat to make it feel less dry.

"Hey Lugnut."

The dog raised his head again.

"Come here."

The dog stared at the boy for a moment. Then opened his mouth in a yawn, revealing his numerous sharp yellow teeth and red tongue, and then laid his head back down.

"Lugnut."

The dog gave no response and turned his gaze to stare at a chair that had suddenly become more interesting. The boy breathed in and out in a huff of frustration. He did not want to walk over to the dog. He wanted the dog to come over to him.

If he walked over to the dog it would mean he had failed. It would mean that the dog called the shots. Also, if he invaded the dog's personal space, he did not know what the dog would do.

The boy's eyes followed the dog's gaze to the chair with its spare wooden frame and blue cushion. He let his eyes drift across the kitchen, taking it all in. Inside, the feeling that he should just get up and go back to the living room to play matchbox cars was slowly growing. The boy's eyes roved across various items. Refrigerator, dishwasher, cupboard doors, toaster oven, sink, bowl of dog treats on the counter. The thoughts of admitting defeat were banished by the creation of a new plan. The boy got up and walked over to the counter. He could feel the dog's eyes following his movements. He picked a single treat, green and bone shaped, from the bowl and went back to sit cross legged in the middle of the room once again.

The dog's head was up and watching with rapt attention. His red tongue licked his black lips in anticipation. His nose worked, testing the air. The boy held the treat in front of himself, holding one end with the tips of his fingers.

"Hey Lugnut."

The red tail beat the floor.

"Come here."

The large paws pushed against the floor, the thick legs raised the great body upwards. The dog stood and stared at the treat, unsure for a second what to do. The indecision was short lived. The dog moved forward, his nails clicking on the linoleum. The dog walked to the boy and gingerly took the treat from the boy's fingers, careful in all his movements. The boy reached out slowly, and put his hand on the dogs side. He tentatively began moving his hand back and forth, rubbing the red fur coat. Each back and forth movement got longer. The boy's fingers moved from the top of the dog's head to the middle of his broad back. The dog sat on his haunches, and raised his nose up towards the sky, his eyes closed, obviously enjoying the attention.

"You're a pretty good dog, aren't ya Lugnut. You just got a bad rap, that's all."

The boy petted the dog for a full minute and then let his hand drop. His point had been proven. He had been victorious in his goal. The boy began to stand. The growl came deep from within the dog's throat. His mouth did not open and he did not show any teeth. It was more a vibration than a sound. More something felt than heard. The dog sat face to face with the boy, his muzzle just inches away from the boy's nose. The boy stared into the gold colored eyes and stood a little more. The dog growled once again in disapproval. The boy sat fully back down, raised a hand, and started to again pet the threatening red bulk before him.

Another minute passed. The boy again lowered his hand. Again the growl from the back of the throat. The boy recommenced his petting. The dog gazed at the boy steadily, reminding the boy of his vulnerability. The dog's tail did not wag. His jaw did not hang slack. He sat perfectly straight and stared at the boy who was now under his control. A petting machine under his command.

The boy was scared. He did not know what to do. He could not bring himself to meet the big dog's eye. The boy's hand moved rhythmically, following the unspoken orders of his new canine master. All of the warnings his mother had given him ran through his head. The constant lectures and reminders breeding uncertainty over what to do. The boy couldn't just quit petting. God only knows what the dog would do if he did. Maybe the dog would just let the boy go, or maybe he would tear his face off. It was a gamble, and he lacked the experience to judge the relative likelihood of each scenario. The boy felt all alone and isolated. He could not get the image of the dog's large yellow teeth out of his head. He could not ignore the relative disparity in their mass and weight.

The boy couldn't call for help. The boy couldn't face his mother's admonishments for doing what she had specifically told him not to do. He could see her lecturing him in front of everybody. He could feel the shame as she made him feel like a little kid in front of everyone whom he wanted to have think the opposite. He could see the disapproving look of his grandparents and uncle. He could see his brothers mocking looks as they relished in him getting in trouble. The boy was stuck. He was trapped. He had no escape.

Minute passed by after minute. Twice more the boy built up the courage to challenge the alpha in its dominance. Twice the quiet growls drove him back to his task of endlessly rubbing the big red dog's back. There was no way out. Nothing he could do. The boy could think of only two solutions, and in his mind the negatives of both were of equal weight, leaving him in limbo. Tears of frustration filled his eyes. He knew the longer that he sat there, endlessly petting the damned dog, the more likely it would be for someone to come into the kitchen and find him. A combination of hope and dread filled him at the thought of such an event.

The boy's arm was becoming tired. The repetitive motion was becoming harder to do, but he dared not slow down. He would have to make a run for it. In a single motion he would have to stop petting and lunge for the doorway, a seemingly far off beacon of escape. He would have to be quick. He would not be able to hesitate. The boy began to brace himself for the lunge. The dog felt the boy's arm stiffen, and sensed his changing stance. The dog leaned in closer to the boy, as though warning him that any attempt to break away would be futile. The boy felt the dog's muscles become more taunt, matching the boy's in readiness for action. The boy's heart beat rapidly in his chest. He uncrossed his legs and put one foot firmly on the floor, ready to push off. The dog raised his back end off of the ground slightly, his body began to shake with anticipation. The boy began to count in his head. In one, two, thr......

"Lugnut, come here boy."

The sound of Uncle Bill's voice filled the house and the dog stood up and trotted out of the kitchen, his tail wagging and tongue lolling out of the side of his mouth. The boy sat and watched him go, breathing deeply and willing his heart to slow its rapid motion. The boy's mother walked into the kitchen and looked down at him as though from a great height.

"What are you doing sitting in the middle of the floor?"

"Nothing, just playing."

"Well, come back in the living room and say goodbye. Uncle Bill is leaving."

"Okay."

# The Green Monster

They call jealousy the green monster. It's something that defies logic. Who is this? What are they doing here? Why are they talking to her? Your stomach twists and tightens into a knot. Your heart begins to pound and adrenaline makes you tense and ready to spring. You feel your breath grow short and rapid. You feel dizzy. Your mind spirals out of control, awash in hormonal chemicals. The things that control such feelings are not directed by your logical mind. They are directed by your primal brain. It's a fear, a dread of a potential loss. To show you how badly you would feel, your brain simulates what the loss will feel like. It's meant to be a motivator, a call to battle to stake claim to what you want, but what happens when you've already lost what you wanted? What happens when it's already gone?

An empty chaotic feeling. A demand to fight for something that is no longer there. What can you do then but sit and stew in your own juices? Sometimes jealousy is a good thing, it forces you to do things that you might not otherwise do. Sometimes jealousy is a bad thing. Sometimes it makes us do things that only makes things worse. Sometimes the situation is real. Sometimes it is only cooked up in our own heads. Mix it in with worry, anxiety, anger, and bitterness, and you create a nightmare.

You shouldn't feel jealousy at something you have already lost. You have no right to. This is what logic tells us. This is the conclusion any rational mind can come to. Unfortunately, jealousy is not hooked to the logical mind. Like so many things it must be overcome. Like so many things the more you feed it and give into it, the larger it becomes.

# The Cowboy

The horse exploded with a loud neigh filled with outrage and fear. Its strangely colored eyes rolled back and its ears fell flat as it struggled to pull back with all its might. The horse struggled to keep its head low, to keep the halter and attached rope from lifting its head. Every muscle in the geldings body was taut. Its lips were peeled back, exposing large yellowed teeth. Its front legs were braced tight on the ground, knees unbent, a counterweight to the force of the rope. The horse pushed off in a sudden burst of energy that lifted its entire body into the air, regaining some of the inches so far lost in the struggle.

Morris leaned against the corral fence and watched the battle in silence. Two men struggled with the beast, desperately trying to force it into the waiting gooseneck trailer which would take it away. The bald one with watery eyes heaved on the rope wrapped tightly in his gloved hands. His brow glistened with sweat and his face shone bright red like an apple for teacher. The rope was stretched through a hole in the side of the trailer around a metal post, and then out the open trailer door to the struggling equine monster. Morris had not known the bald one was bald when he had arrived. The bald one's black cowboy hat, with its redtail hawk feather in the band, lay trampled in the dirt. The first casualty.

Behind the horse the skinny one raised and lowered a long leather strap rhythmically, each fall of the strap bringing a sharp crack across the horse's rump. The skinny one had mean squinty eyes which he hid under his pulled low straw hat, it's brim turned up like a smile on a cheshire cat. His pearl snap shirt was undone halfway to his navel, exposing a bony chest. His shirt tails hung free of his pants, hiding the belt buckle that declared him the best saddle bronc rider at some two bit local rodeo. Curses flowed from the skinny one's mouth in a steady unending stream which echoed off the nearby hills. Each word part of a vile sonnet, with the crack of the strap keeping a steady beat.

With each snap the bald man gave the rope a jerk. Slowly, inch by inch, dragging the horse into the trailer. Sometimes the horse would brace its legs and lunge back, regaining some of what had been lost, but it was slowly losing the battle. Dust filled the air of the corral around the horse's legs. It's body flailed about, refusing with every fiber of its being to give up its stubborn fight. It was not enough. The loose rope behind the bald man continued to get longer and longer.

A third man, the fat one, sat in the shade next to the watering trough. His fancy western shirt was ripped. Dust and dirt coated one entire side of his body, masking the once vivid colors of his ruined shirt and obscuring half of his face. His flat topped cowboy hat was tipped back and sweat ran from his curly hair, creating small rivers in the grit. His ponderous belly rose and fell rapidly. His breath wheezed through his fumanchu moustache, as he struggled to take in enough oxygen. His piggish eyes were half closed, staring out at the action.

The fat one had been the second casualty of the day.  As the horse had struggled to be loaded the men had lost their tempers and the fat one had moved in to give the gelding a slap across its backside.  The horse had moved so quickly that Morris doubted that the hand had even hit before the fat man had found himself on the ground, put there courtesy of a fast moving back hoof.  The fat man had laid on his side in the dirt for a few moments, before dragging himself into the shade next to the watering trough.  The other two men had watched him in silence.  It had been then that the skinny one had pulled the strap out from behind the seat of the pickup.

Morris adjusted his ball cap, Kessler Bulls emblazoned across the front, and struggled to keep himself from leaping over the fence into the corral to join the action.  His t-shirt hung wet against his body with sweat.  It was a hot day, and not a single cloud offered relief from the relentless assault of the bright sun hanging in the empty sky.  He had been out all morning, laying handline in a dusty field, preparing to bring water to a thirsty crop.  Helping to boost the growth of hay to feed to the cattle through the winter.  That was where the old man had found him.  Kicking the piled pipes to make sure that no rattlesnakes lurked inside.

"Drop what you're doing," the old man had barked.  "I've sold that goddamn horse and they're coming to pick him up today."

"Yes sir."  Morris had replied immediately.  The old man was a stickler about respect.  "Pardon me for asking sir, but who the hell would want to buy Copper?"

"Who?"

The old man never named his horses.

"Copper, the horse, who in the hell would want to buy him?"

"Some rodeo fella.  Don't worry.  I told him everything. Seems he's looking for some rough stock to train on.  Go put the halter on him with a long lead rope. You now how much that son of a bitch hates getting loaded. Take him to the corral."

"You want me to stay at the corral and help load him?"

"What? You want to go up and play cowboy instead of getting this work done? These damn pipes won't lay out themselves."

"It shouldn't take long. They might need an extra set of hands."

"I warned him that that horse is a real mother. He's supposed to be bringing along a couple of pals to help get the bastard loaded."

"You know how difficult Copper can get. One more will likely make things go a little quicker. Plus it would probably be good to have someone there to make sure they don't kill him before they pay for him."

The old man had stood silent and eyed Morris for a few seconds. His beady eyes had moved up and down Morris's lanky frame. Finally a thin slip of a smile poked past the old man's gray moustache.

"Whatever. Just get these pipes going on the Maidment fields before the end of the day. That orchard grass isn't going to grow itself."

"Yes sir. I will sir."

The old man had hated Copper from the first time he had tried to ride him. He had gotten the horse for a steal and felt proud of himself about it, often bragging to the other old ranchers who spent part of each morning at the Dinty Cafe. Copper was a well muscled buckskin colored horse with a white stripe down his nose. The old man had spotted Copper at an auction when he was selling some old open cows. The man riding him in the ring had put him through his paces with ease. The rider had climbed off over the horse's rump and given its tail a jerk for good measure. The rider had then walked around, picking up all four feet, and then jerked on the horse's ears just to show that nothing would bother the animal.

The old man knew good horse flesh when he saw it. Sure the horse had a couple scars on its hide, including a deep one across the center of its forehead, but it had four good feet, acted surefooted, and appeared to be only five years old. The fact that it was gentle as a lamb was just icing on the cake. Sure, many avoided the horse because of the scars, but the old man knew a deal when he saw one.

The old man had often quipped, "he's probably the best horse looking horse I've ever bought. What's a few scars but a bit of decoration?"

The old man's tune had changed the first time he had tried to saddle his new purchase. The buckskin horse had shied back and then jerked its head so hard that the lead rope had snapped like it was made of string. The horse had bolted out of the barn, knocking the old man flat as it went. A few more attempts soon made it apparent that the old man's deal of a lifetime had actually been a scam.

The old man had spit and raged for days. "I'm going to kill those sons of a bitches. Only a rotten mother butes a horse at an auction."

The old man had called up everyone involved in the transaction that he could find, but there was nothing he could do. Everyone he talked to gave him the same spiel. A few sympathetic words, and then a firm reminder that all sales were final.

"God damn tranquilizer using bastards. What if someone had bought him for a kids horse? They all belong in the bowels of god damn hell."

The old man had found himself stuck. Trying to make the best of a bad situation, he had tried to break the horse of its bad habits, but after the fourth time of catching a glancing blow from a hoof he had decided it was no longer worth his time. After the last attempt the old man had left the barn muttering about the glue factory.

Morris liked the look of the horse. The old man had been right. It was a good looking piece of horse flesh. Morris had named the horse Copper because of the color of its eyes, like molten metal. The old man never named his horses. He at most would point out the buckskin one, or the dun one, or the one with the two white feet. Morris had private names for all of them. It had taken him several days after the last incident before he got up the courage to talk to the old man.

"Would you mind if I tried working with Copper?"

"What?"

"The buckskin horse."

"That son of a bitch. Why would you want to bother with him?"

"I think he'd be a pretty good horse if I just worked with him a bit. I'll only do it in the evening after all my work is done."

The old man had studied him for a bit and then gave one of his rare smiles, barely visible under his moustache.

"Look kid. I know what you're thinking. Been there myself a time or two. But a horse like that is never going to be quite right. Someone treated that horse bad and its gone through too much crap to ever be okay again. It's never going to be worth a damn. I'm going to sell the bastard and that's going to be the end of it."

It had taken two months to find a buyer. The old man wouldn't lie about the horse. He wouldn't screw someone over the same way he had been.

The horse neighed wildly again. The cursing of the skinny one reached a crescendo and the pace of the swinging leather strap increased. Each crack was accentuated by the scream of the stubborn horse. Morris watched, wondering if the skinny man's arm would ever grow tired. The skinny man's little mean eyes glittered, and Morris could swear he saw the glint of a smile on his thin lips.

Morris thought about climbing over the fence and taking the strap to the skinny man and seeing how he liked it, but he stayed where he was and did nothing. Imagination and reality are often two different animals. It was easy to see himself knocking the skinny man to the ground, but such an outcome seemed unlikely. The men on the other side of the fence outclassed him in both size and numbers, and undoubtedly the old man would not take kindly to his hired hand fighting with men willing to buy the troublesome horse. Morris felt his hands clench tight in anger and frustration.

The bald man was tiring. With each crack of the strap he still gave the rope a jerk, but each jerk was becoming weaker than the last. He lifted his arm, still holding the rope, to wipe the sweat from his eyes. It was bad timing. The horse lunged back with all of its might. The bald man was caught off balance. His body slammed into the side of the gooseneck trailer with a metallic bang. The rope came loose from his hands and the horse, sensing it was free, turned and ran to the far side of the corral, trailing the long rope behind it. The bald one leaned against the trailer. Doubled over in pain.

"Shit. I think the son of a bitch broke my thumb."

The skinny one stood staring at the horse, breathing hard, the leather strap hanging limp from his hand. His mouth curled, voicing silent curses. His mean little eyes turned and looked at Morris.

"Hey, why the hell are you just sitting there instead of helping you little asshole. Aren't you a real cowboy?"

Morris looked at the three cowboys in the corral. The fat one sitting in the dust wheezing, the bald one doubled over fighting back tears, and the skinny one sweating from his exertions. The finery that marked them as who they were was in tatters. Morris looked and then turned his back on the ugly scene, walking away.

"I guess not," he said over his shoulder.

Morris went back to his irrigation pipes and got back to work setting them out in their straight line across the dry field. After half an hour he saw the three cowboys drive past down the gravel road, their dually pickup and empty gooseneck trailer kicking dust into the air behind them. All three men sat staring straight forward, their expressions blank. Morris watched until they disappeared up the hill and then got back to work. He had promised the water would be running by the end of the day.

The old man came by right as the sprinkler heads began to clack and spin, shooting water onto the field by the dying light of the setting sun.

"Why is that damn horse still here?"

"They couldn't get him loaded."

"God damn that son of a bitch. I'm guessing they won't be back. Can hardly blame them. Get that damn halter off him and kick him back out with the rest. You can go home once you're done."

"Yes sir."

Morris found the horse where it had been left in the far corner of the corral. Morris picked up the rope and gently gave it a pull. Copper followed quietly. Morris led Copper down into the horse pen, next to the old barn which contained all the saddles and tack. He took the halter off and went into the barn. He came back out with a can of oats and a curry comb. Copper knickered in the half light. Morris set the can of oats where Copper could reach it and started combing the dust and dead hair from the horse's coat, just as he had done every night for the past two months. He was careful to avoid the fresh wounds. The horse knickered again and ate its oats.

# Molly

Fucking. This is probably the best place to start the story. Her body folded, legs on my shoulders, breasts bouncing in time with my thrusts, her cunt wet. I don't know why women don't like the word cunt. Why cunt is such a bad word compared to pussy, or vagina, or taco? I like the word cunt. It's short and succinct. It doesn't deserve to be banished to a lexiconian hell. Her hair is a dark brown, nearly black, and slightly curly. Her eyes are brown. Her face sharp. She has the bottom half of a frog, thin legs, no ass. Nice round tits, shapely nipples, a soft belly. All of this I see through the windows of my eyes as my body's energy and power push her off of the old mattress onto the floor. It's a short drop, no frame or bed spring.

I keep going. I can't stop. I can't culminate. We slide around the room like a bulldozer, sweeping away dirty clothes and discarded books. I can't concentrate. My body is on automatic. Its sweat drips onto her as it fucks. I can feel everything, cunt, legs, breasts, her hands on my back, cool air blowing across me from an open window, but I'm disconnected, I'm not really there. I'm happy to be there, but it's more for the satisfaction of my body's needs than my own. My mind won't shut down, it's distracting my body.

Her name is Molly. Names though aren't important. If you changed someone's name it doesn't change who they are. We could call her Morgan, or Millie, or even Jacob. Names are just placeholders, ways to identify through speech and word. Her hands tighten around my body, urging it on, beseeching it to cross the finish line. My body's fingers clench her ass, tips tickled by the short dark hairs that grow in its crack.

The woman beneath my body, this woman that they call Molly, begins to groan louder. She starts to shudder. Her legs tighten around my body's neck and she begins to spasm with ripples of delight. Deep animalistic sounds escape from her throat as she's carried away by a wave of pleasure. She's a little ball of ecstasy beneath my body. Her entire form tightens with the force of her orgasm, every muscle tenses, and then relaxes, collapsing with the release.

My body doesn't stop. It continues to pump away. She begins to tighten again. She moans, both wanting my body to stop and wanting my body to continue. She's tired, she's been up in the air for some time. Her cunt runs dry, unable to keep up with the continued fucking. Each thrust is accompanied by more friction. Pleasure slowly turns to pain. The feel of my body's thrusting dick in her cunt changes. My body feels wetness directly on the shaft. The condom has ripped. My body pulls out of her and exhaustion overtakes me. My body collapses on top of her and she breathes rapidly and deeply in its ear, rubbing its back as though it's a well trained beast who has done well.

We lay there for a while, regathering our strength. Slowly the two halves of myself come back together. The strange sensation of being a spectator ceases. We stand up, rubbing dirt off of our arms, legs, and torsos. I pull off the ripped condom, empty, and throw it in the general direction of the trashcan. The two of us climb back onto the mattress and she lays in the cusp of my arm. My balls ache, over primed without release. I adjust how they hang between my legs so I'm more comfortable. Not a word is said between us, our bodies are entwined but our minds are separate, both lost in our own little worlds of worries, hopes, and dreams. We fall asleep without saying a word to each other.

The next morning we shower together and I jerk off on her leg as she nuzzles my chest and juggles my balls with her fingers. Culmination at last, a combination of pain and ecstasy. We say little as we rub ourselves dry with the same towel and get dressed. She follows me to the front door of the old house. We stand for a moment, staring at each other. Feeling awkward, I open the door, take a step, and turn back. In my mind I try to form words to say something to put some kind of meaning to everything beyond a physical need. Nothing comes to mind. I walk down to my car as she closes the door behind me. She watches from the window as I get in and drive away.

She walks down the stairs, the old boards creaking beneath her bare feet. She's ready for bed. Pajama pants, tank top, a pair of oval shaped glasses she wasn't wearing earlier that evening. She walks by on light feet and rounds the corner to the kitchen and bathroom. She doesn't notice that I'm not asleep. We're the only people awake in the house. First floor, second floor, basement. Beds, futons, and mattresses on the ground. All filled with slumbering revelers.

I'm drunk. I'm laying on an old beat up couch, its springs creaking beneath me with every movement, its well worn cushions smelling of age and mildew, its wooden frame peaking through a worn out cover. It had been a good party. I'm glad that I came. It had been unexpected when Denise had walked up to me at the Hash and invited me to come to a party being held at her house. It was a nice gesture. It had been a long time since I'd been invited to a real party. Beer, liquor, and drunken revelry. Every room and corner containing a new group of people, a new conversation to listen to or join. Jokes, opinions, drama, derision. It had been a long time.

I lay in the dark, my head in the clouds but my body not yet ready to drop into dormancy. I lay there in the front room and listen to the sounds of the sleeping house around me. I hear the toilet flush and footsteps growing louder as she rounds the corner. She pulls up even with the couch. I raise my head.

"Have a good night."

She jumps a little, startled by the sudden noise in the silent house. Her sharp features turn to look down at me.

"I didn't know anyone was still awake."

"I haven't fallen asleep yet. Still have a little too much energy."

"I was just using the bathroom."

My first thought is to say that I know. The flushing toilet is always a dead giveaway, but I don't. Saying such things is a social faux pas, a mistake that marks you as being weird, a social outcast who can't play the game of life because they don't understand the rules. Instead I take a different tact.

"That was a fun party tonight."

She smiles down at me. It looks awkward, like she doesn't do it often. Her sharp features become even more defined and for a moment her eyes twinkle in the night.

"I usually don't like these big social gatherings, but I had a good time tonight too."

She stops smiling, and her face regains its normal shape of distant neutrality and disinterest. "Well, good night."

"Good night."

Her footsteps recede back up the stairs and I hear her bedroom door open and close. My thoughts slowly wind their way through the memories of the party. She's a strange woman, aloof, a spectator. I had met her just that night. She was one of Denise's roommates. It's only rarely that I could be called the life of the party. I'm not that kind of person. I'm a distant person, a spectator myself in many ways, but not that night. That night I was somebody to be remembered. That night my desperation for social interaction combined with copious amounts of alcohol had overcome my inhibitions and self-doubt. That night I could do no wrong. I could talk to anybody. None of my jokes fell flat. None of the things I said seemed weird. I was cool. I was confident. I was witty. I was suave. I could do anything.

When I had first arrived I was introduced around by Denise to the non-hashers and the hashers I didn't know. Molly had been one of the non-hashers. A new drunken friend pointed her out in the crowd. He described her as antisocial and a ball buster. She preferred to be left alone. If you said the wrong thing to her she was likely to take a swing at you. I took my friend's opinion with a grain of salt. He seemed like the type who had people take swings at him on a fairly regular basis. I looked at Molly as he spoke. She was an attractive woman, all the parts in the right shapes and proportions. The advice on her reputation only added to the physical pull.

Molly spent a large amount of the party upstairs in her room. Out of sight and out of mind. When she was downstairs she always seemed to be slightly separated from the rest. She would stand in corners and only talk to people that she knew, or stand just outside the circle of conversation, listening to the banter, but not wanting to intrude. I'm not usually sure of myself. I'm not usually cocky. I'm not usually brave. This time I was. Sometimes you can be anything. Sometimes you get a taste of your full potential. When I saw her standing outside the circle I turned and started talking to her, dragging her into the conversation, forcing her to be part of the group. She was a fairly interesting person when you could actually get her talking.

The sound of the door opening and closing. Footsteps on the stairs once again. My eyes follow her as she comes walking down. Feet, legs, belly, breasts, head. My eyes trace her curves as she appears. I notice that she's not wearing a bra. I notice that her tank top can't hide her hardened nipples. She walks by the couch again.

"You're back."

"Just getting a drink of water."

"Hmmm."

She continues on her way into the kitchen, a tension hanging in the air. I feel a primal urge well up inside of me. I feel a need, an animalistic voice calling out. Get up from this couch. Follow her into the kitchen. Grab that woman. Kiss her. The kitchen light flicks on. I hear the sound of the cupboard opening and the scrape of a glass as its pulled from the shelf. I hear the faucet turn on, the sounds of a glass filling and then emptying down a throat. The voice in my head rails against me. God damn it you coward. What are you doing? This is your chance. Be daring for once in your life. Don't just sit there wishing, actually do something. I ignore the voice. I think to myself that it's being stupid. She'll think I'm creepy. She'll think I'm weird. She'll tell everybody that I'm a creepy weird dude. It's been a long time, and the times I was daring before have been few and far between.

The light in the kitchen turns out and her footsteps precede back into the living room on their way to the stairs. She brushes by the couch again. I smile.

"Be careful, before you know it you're going to have to go to the bathroom again."

She smiles down at me.

"Good night again."

"Good night again."

She moves back up the stairs and her door opens and closes. You cowardly piece of shit. The voice is not willing to let this go. There's no denying it. There was a basic feeling, a primal draw, a sub-conscious call. My body begins to quiver, fueled by a rage over my inability to meet its pent up needs. What-ifs, probablys, probably nots, they all run through my head. You asshole, you sorry son of a bitch. What do they have to do, put up a fucking billboard? How can it be any more obvious? How can you be such a fool? I have doubts. My body doesn't want to listen. It doesn't see this as a matter of logic, problem solving, or intellectual thoughts. This is a thing of gut feelings and instinct. You're a pussy. That's why you never get laid. That's why you never get the girl, because you're a pussy.

It doesn't matter now. My body is right. I am a pussy. I am a coward. I am a fool. I over think everything and therefore miss everything. It doesn't matter now. My chance is gone. The opening has closed. I saw a possibility and turned away. I don't deserve anything, not if I can't reach out and take it when it's right in front of me. My mind is filled with partial relief that the chance is gone, part disgust at not taking it, and part sadness that I've missed yet another moment. There's nothing I can do. My self-doubts have won again. The chance is past.

The sound of a door opening and closing. My heartbeat quickens. Footsteps again on the stairs. Again a figure slowly emerges into view, each step revealing a little more from the bottom up. She pauses by the couch and looks down at me.

"I needed another drink of water."

She gives me the look, head slightly bent down, eyes peering through her lashes with a hungry and intense gaze, and walks towards the kitchen. I feel something within me snap. My body takes control, kicking my mind out of the driver's seat. I feel my body rise from the couch. I feel it move forward step by step. I'm just a passenger on this ride. My body turns and enters the light of the kitchen. Molly looks at me and I can feel my lips move.

"I could also use some water."

Wordlessly she moves to get another glass, fills it, and hands it to me. I feel my arm lift the glass to my lips, and water flow into my mouth and down my throat. She puts her glass in the sink and we stand looking at each other, then looking away, then looking at each other again. Tension building. Hunger in the air. My arm lowers the half full glass and puts it on the counter. My body takes a step forward. I stare into her eyes and neither one of us look away, electricity in the air.

How does it happen? How do you move from one point to another? No matter how many times I go through it, I still can't say for certain. One moment, staring, moving closer. The next, embraced in each other's arms. Kissing, groping, exploring. Our bodies entangled. I push her until her back is against the cupboard door. My mouth and tongue explore her lips, her neck, her ears. She lets out a quiet involuntary moan. She tastes like cigarettes, but I don't care. Her breath is quick and raspy. I feel the rapid rise and fall of my own chest. My heart thunders in my ears. My hands move as though they are independent, groping her shoulders, back, and buttocks. Both hands grip her low and lift and suddenly she's airborne, legs wrapped around me. Elation, excitement, swimming in glory. Emanating heat against my crotch. I feel myself stiffen, yearn to be free. I am man, hear me roar.

Her legs unwrap and fall back to the floor. She pushes me away from her, keeping her arms stiff to keep me at a distance.

"Not here. Not now."

My conscious mind begins to re-emerge. The animal in me rumbles in disappointment and confusion.

"What? Why?"

"I don't want to wake anyone up. I don't want anybody to hear."

"Okay, okay."

We break apart, breathing hard, and stand looking at each other from a few feet away.

"Can I call you sometime?"

"Yes."

She turns and digs in a drawer for a pen. She walks over and writes her number on my hand.

"I'll call you tomorrow."

"Okay."

She puts the pen away and turns off the kitchen light. We walk back into the living room. She goes up the stairs and I lay back down on the couch. Her door opens and closes. Part of me wants to climb the stairs after her, but the voice tells me that I've done enough. Logic takes hold once more. There are more people sleeping upstairs, more people sleeping in her room. This is not the time or place. Confidence and satisfaction course through my being. I fall asleep smiling like an idiot.

I awake the next morning still grinning. Molly and her cousin stand over me. My eyes aren't open, but I can hear her cousin's voice.

"Why is he smiling like that?"

I hear footsteps as they head into the kitchen. It's early, far too early to already be up and about. I open my eyes and sit up. My socks and shoes sit right where I left them. They go back on my feet. My mind still hazy from sleep I make my goodbyes and head out into the cool March air. I get into my car and start the engine, wait for the defroster to do the minimal amount of work required, and drive home. I feel triumphant. I can do anything.

Home. I'm joining some friends for breakfast. I get in the shower without thinking. My hands are on the faucets before the little light blinks in my head. I get out, grab my cell phone, and copy down the number on my hand. Add new contact: Molly. I shower, brush my teeth, and put on new clothes. Smiling to myself I go outside and walk over to my friends' place a few doors down. We make small talk and get in their car and head out for breakfast. I don't usually talk much about my personal life, but this time I'm anxious to be able to brag about my victory. I keep it classy. I don't give too many details, but I share my excitement. I feel good, it's nice to know that you're capable of doing such things. It's nice to surprise yourself every now and again.

We wait in line for about an hour. By the time we're seated the timing would suggest something more akin to brunch than breakfast, though in all fairness, no one has ever been able to convincingly tell me when one ends and the other begins. The food is good. My friends and I sit and talk about nothing, just babble about recent happenings and fresh news. Small talk, light conversation, whatever you want to call it.

By the time we get done eating the brunch crowd has started to move on and the tide of the lunch crowd has started to rise. I can't wait any longer. I'm too excited. I go and stand around the edge of the building, a quiet corner where I can privately build myself up enough to make the call. Get myself positive, get myself calm. Last night I had fought a demon and won, it was time to claim my reward. It's a strange sensation. You can have your tongue in someone's mouth the night before and feel nervous about calling them in the morning. It's the fear of the unknown. My fingers quiver a bit as I open the phone and click through it. Contacts, Molly, dial. The phone begins to ring. I swallow nervously and rehearse what I'm going to say, hoping she won't be able to tell how nervous I am over the phone.

"Hello."

"Hey, it's Shawn."

"Who?"

"Shawn, the guy from last night."

"Who?"

"The guy you made out with last night?"

"Who the fuck is this?"

"We made out in your kitchen."

"I have no fucking idea who you are."

The female voice on the other end disconnects. I feel my body shake with pent up nervousness, now suddenly flooded by fatigue and disappointment. What the hell? What the hell just happened? I make the phone connect again. It rings. It rings. It rings. Hope rises up within me. It was just a mistake, it was all just some kind of mistake. The same female voice answers the phone.

"Hello."

"Is this Molly?"

"Who?"

"Is this Molly's phone?"

"No."

The phone goes silent again. I feel myself deflate. The gears in my mind start turning fast enough to catch up with my present situation. I consider dialing the number again, but quickly ignore the impulse as being ridiculous. The woman on the other end of the phone is clearly not Molly. The phone number she gave me was not hers. Molly gave me a fake phone number. For a moment I wonder if she had written it down wrong, but it doesn't seem likely. For a moment I wonder if I had entered it into my contacts wrong, but I remember double and triple checking. No. Fake phone number, that's the most probable and reasonable likelihood. My reward is fool's gold.

Going from such a high to such a low in the space of a minute is tiring. I feel myself sag. I feel my body shrink to a smaller size. I'm despondent and depressed. I walk back around the corner and get into the waiting car to take me home. My friends' hopeful faces turn dour when they see mine. They don't need to ask how it went, but I tell them anyways.

"Fake number."

Words of comfort. I don't really hear them. What the hell happened? It seemed like everything had gone so well. It seemed like she really enjoyed being around me. Did I creep her out? Was she just trying to get away from me? Did I scare her? I'm frustrated and saddened. All that build up just to have it all come to nothing.

When we get home I go back into my apartment and try to go about my day. Things still have to be done. The dishwasher needs unloading and my laundry is piling up. Groceries need to be purchased and the floor could use a good sweeping. I do a few of these things, but mostly lay on my bed, questions running through my head. What the hell? What the fuck? I hate the feeling of inaction, I hate the feeling of not being able to find out the answers to my questions. I'm full of pent up energy, my mind is spinning rapidly, and there's no way to get it to stop. My hands open up my phone. They look at the number listed under her name. They're the digits I remember entering. My fingers click the keypad. I look at my call log. Today, two outgoing calls, both to Melissa.

Melissa. The calls were to Melissa, not Molly. Melissa is an old friend of mine from college, but I probably haven't talked to her in four years. I'm not even sure why she's still in my phone. Disgust at my own stupidity is quickly replaced by excitement. I called Melissa, not Molly. I'm nervous as I press in the commands again. Contacts, Molly, make double sure it is Molly, dial. I feel nervous and apprehensive. I swear if this is a fake number the heavens are going to owe me an answer for why they like to fuck with me so much. Ring. Ring. Ring. Somebody picks up.

"Hello."

I recognize the voice.

"Hey, it's Shawn."

"Hey, how are you doing?"

She sounds nervous too.

"Good, good. Yourself?"

I hope I sound confident, not nervous.

"Pretty good, a little hungover, but overall not bad."

"So, I was just calling to see if you would like to get a beer or something tomorrow afternoon?"

"Sure, what time?"

Shit, I should have thought about this before I called.

"Ummmm, how about three?"

"Can we make it three-thirty?"

"Sure."

"Where do you want to go?"

Crap, I really should have thought about this more.

"Let me think about it. You want me to pick you up at your house?"

A pause. Was I being too forward? Was I being creepy for offering?

"Sure, that would be fine."

Relief.

"Great, I'll see you tomorrow then."

"See you tomorrow."

The phone disconnects. I lay back on my bed, smiling like a loon. It's been a long day. I feel like I've been jerked around a little too much by the forces of the universe, but it all worked out in the end. I get up and go about doing the things that need to get done that day to keep my life in some kind of semblance of order.

I spend the morning of my date cleaning my car. Driving down to the nearest car wash. Washing and waxing the outside. Vacuuming the inside and throwing out the random pieces of trash that have collected. Receipts, a newspaper from a couple months ago, a snickers wrapper, and a few old stale cheese puffs that I briefly consider popping in my mouth before deciding against it and throwing them in the garbage. My car isn't a very nice car. It's not expensive or fancy. It doesn't have leather seats or all the new bells and whistles. It's paint is scratched and chipped. The interior is stained. Even though it's a turd I polish it up as best I can. This is the first date I've been on in nine months. I'm nervous.

I'm not good at dates. At least that's what I've always told myself. I never went on many during college, and after college was over I continued making excuses to avoid them. I use to tell people that the reason I never dated was because I didn't feel like it. That I was having too much fun being single to ever bother with it. I didn't want to get myself tied down. These were of course all lies. I had avoided dating for so long because I was scared to date. I was scared to put myself out there, let somebody get to know me. I was scared of all the possibilities that it might entail, of all the possibilities it would close off. I was scared of being rejected. I was scared of all the possible pain.

It's the middle of the afternoon when I drive down to the old house to pick up Molly. The street is split down the middle by a thin layer of grass and trees. Pass the big park on the right, down one more block, and turn to the left. I pull up in front of the house. It's a big white two story structure from the turn of the century, a large covered porch decorated with Buddhist prayer flags and a small lawn in the front. She's waiting on the porch, talking with her cousin. I open my door and step out, waving hello. I watch her jog down the steps and we exchange hellos as she gets into the car. I turn to get back in. My eye catches the eye of her cousin, still sitting on the porch. For just a second our eyes lock, and then we both look away. I get in the car and smile at Molly, put the car in gear, and we head out.

I take her to Prost, a German theme pub on Mississippi Avenue a little ways away. A group of friends took me there just a few nights before. The decorum had seemed about right for a first date, not too trashy, but not too flashy. We sit and sip at our beers, neither one wanting to finish before the other. The talk is light fluff floating between us up into the air, inconsequential, the words back and forth unimportant. It's the little stuff that we fill the world with every day and forget about the next morning so we can talk about it all again. It's a steady filling of silence, both of us guarded, not yet willing to talk about things that actually matter.

When two people go on a date it should be mutually agreed that both will drink a beer before they meet. The start of the date is always an awkward time. Both people put themselves on their best behavior, neither one wanting to break the ice and start showing the things that make them weird, the things that make people interesting. It isn't until the second beer that the walls start to come down. It isn't until the second beer that people start showing their true selves.

We're halfway through the second beer when Molly starts to pull things out of her purse, looking for chapstick. Out onto the table come all the usual items. Wallet, keys, a pair of sunglasses, gum. Amongst the usual is a small three by four notebook with a black cover. Something unusual. Something I instantly recognize. An opening.

"I have that exact same notebook."

"What?"

"I have that exact same notebook, only mine has an orange cover."

She gives me a look which reads so what.

"I use it to write down things when they randomly jump into my head, so I won't forget them."

Her look turns into a combination of surprise and bemusement. She puts the items back into her purse, but stops to look at the small notebook.

"That's what I use it for too. What do you put in it?"

"Little sayings, ideas for inventions, economic theories, philosophy. Lots of stuff."

For the first time in the date she seems to be entirely focused on me.

"Wow. I don't put anything like that in mine."

"What do you put in it?"

"Stories, poems, sometimes some pictures that my friends draw."

She opens the book and shows me a ink pen picture of a girl drawn on one of the pages.

"My friend Jess drew that."

"Nice. What kind of stories do you write?"

"Most of it's pretty dark. I never let anybody read it. Most of it's probably pretty fucked up."

"Maybe you'll let me read some of it sometime?"

Her face contorts into a momentary look of panic before quickly changing back to neutral. There's something dark about her. She's interesting to talk to, but she doesn't smile much. She puts off a strange vibe, as though she's always in hiding.

"Probably not. I don't let anybody read what I write."

I sense that I've gone too far, that maybe I've pushed a button that I shouldn't have.

"Okay. I used to write a lot myself when I was a kid. Stopped doing it when I was in college. Just got too busy I guess."

I smile, trying to smooth over the pothole that we've hit. Her phone chimes and she takes it out and reads a text. She smiles to herself. I watch in silence and do my best to hide my curiosity. She texts something back and looks back up at me.

"Everything okay?"

"Yeah. Me and my roommates just have an agreement to text each other when we're out on a date. If the date isn't going well then you text back clown. Then they'll call you to give you an excuse to get out of there. If things are going well you just text back elephant."

"Which one am I?"

"Elephant."

The day moves on. We leave the bar and walk down the street to a nearby restaurant to get some food. Everything on the street is meant to look like a hole in the wall establishment, though all the people inside are modern and trendy. As we talk our words gain more weight. We talk about little stories and factoids from our respective lives. Things that our friends have known about us for years, but to each other are new, funny, and interesting. I enjoy her company. It's a good first date. Evening begins to arrive and I drive her back home, passing through the shadows cast by the trees that grow in the middle of the street.

We sit in the car a while, talk a little more, and then make our goodbyes. As she starts to step out of the car I stop her. I want to kiss her again. I want to feel the heat again. I want to feel the passion. I don't. Instead we hug and I just smile.

"I had a good time this afternoon."

"Me too."

"Can I see you again?"

"Yes."

She gets out of the car and walks toward her house. She turns once and I wave goodbye. She waves back. I drive away. My car meanders through the city streets, but I float high amongst the clouds.


I call after a couple days. Her phone goes to voicemail. I leave a message after the beep.

"Hey, it's Shawn. Just seeing if you'd like to go get dinner sometime."

Silence. I try again a few days later. This time she picks up.

"Hello?"

"Hi, it's Shawn. I was just calling to see if you'd like to get dinner this week."

"No."

"Maybe another time?"

"No. I don't think I want to see you again." The call is cut off from her end.

Confusion, hurt, anger. I don't understand. The first date seemed to go so well. What the hell just happened? I have a sixteen year old's understanding of women. Such complexities as this are beyond me.

Work, play, time, it all blends together and months pass. I mostly forget about it. However, sometimes I can't sleep. I tend to my body's needs, but there's no way to masturbate the mind. These are the weak times. These are the strange times. These are the times you think of things and people you never think about any other time. A midnight text.

*Why?*

I sit in my bed and wish I could snatch it back. I put my phone down and roll over. The silence of the night is broken by the buzz of my phone. An answer.

*I don't know.*

Silence.

Spring gives way to early summer. Things get warmer and life continues on much as it always has. It's a warm day in June when Denise comes up to me at the Hash run and invites me to her birthday party. I'm nervous. I don't know whether or not I should go. I haven't been back since the last day I dropped off Molly. It doesn't really seem to matter. I agree to come.

I show up the night of the party. Things are already in full swing. I go in and take an offered beer. Molly is there, standing in a corner, talking to people she knows, just like last time. I don't care. I drink, I joke, I laugh, and I have a good time. I don't avoid Molly. We both go to the keg at the same time. I say hello. She replies. We start talking. No questions pertaining to the past. Only now, just the present. If I was sober

I'd probably ask questions. What the hell was up with that crap three months ago? I'm not sober. I don't ask. She gives me a look, the meaning of which is implanted deep within my genes. The body sounds its klaxons and prepares.

The night winds down, Molly and I sit on that same old musty couch, talking about nothing. Everyone else is asleep. The hardest part of such situations is always moving two people from talking to what they really want to do. The mind must silence its doubts and fears, kick back, and let the body take control. The body is an instinctual creature, it knows what it's doing. I can never remember when this happens. It just does. We embrace, we kiss, we rub against each other. Our bodies are ready while our minds are still debating. I nibble on her earlobes, neck, and collarbone. Her shirt is pulled up, her bra pulled down. I suck her nipples. Her breath comes harder and she moans. I reach for her pants, she pulls away from me. Her face shows signs of fear.

"What is it?"

"You're probably too cool to care, but I have herpes and HPV."

I should care, but I don't. My body aches with its needs. It's been a long time, such a long time. I'm undecided, my mind abstaining, voting neither yay or nay. My body wins the vote by default.

"I don't care."

I carry her upstairs. With each footstep the protests of my mind fall farther behind. You don't know this person. What the hell happened three months ago? Don't you realize the risk? Is this a risk you want to take for someone you don't even know? My body doesn't listen. My body doesn't care. My body doesn't understand concepts beyond the here and now. I close the door to her room behind us. Bookcases line the wall, a mattress sits on the floor with no frame, the window is slightly open. Our clothes fall from our bodies, freed from entwining fabrics hiding the nudity beneath. We're tangled together, seeking to become one. My mind makes one last protest to stop and think and then my fingers enter her wetness and her hand wraps around my dick. Heavy breathing and moans.

"Fuck me."

"Do you have condoms?"

"Yes, in the top drawer of the dresser."

The connection is broken as I get up and walk over to the dresser. My brain screams at me, but it's from a great distance away. My body is in full control now. This isn't an act of love, it's purely an act of the physical. A bodily need that can't be met any other way.

I kneel back on the mattress with her legs to either side. I fumble with the condom, put it on the wrong way so it won't unroll, turn it over, and pull it down. My hands are shaking. She watches me with her deep brown eyes. I struggle to get it in. It's been so long. Probably close to two years. Her hands guide the shaft. Warmth and wetness. In and out, harder, harder, slip out, fumble to get it back in, start again. Ecstasy.

I look down at her as I thrust, the target of my lust, and feel nothing. I know nothing about her beyond a few small facts and her willingness to fuck. All the rest is just pure fantasy. The conjuring of a fevered dream that doesn't include love and laughter, simply the illusion of flesh and bone better suited to the task of providing needed pleasure compared to the hand which I've long relied on. She's not a person to me, simply an object. I feel the surge of conquest, the giddiness of finally breaking the long dry spell. All emotions for myself, but nothing for the receptacle that is the woman moaning beneath me.

I look down at her and her eyes have no warmth, no caring, just cold instinctual pleasure. I know if I looked in a mirror I'd see the same in my own eyes. This isn't an act beyond anything but the primal. Two drunken bodies out of the control of their minds, masturbating into each other. Brought together just by attraction and availability. I look down and realize she herself is not the goal, but just the wetness between her legs.

What is this? What am I doing? Part of me wants to stop, pull out, and flee. Why am I taking such risks? I don't pull out. I don't flee. I stay right where I am. Humping away like mad. The risk has already been taken. The deed has already started. Why stop now? My mind breaks loose and flees. I sit in a chair across the room, no longer truly part of the action, and watch my body thrust itself desperately into her.

# Rant Of A Snarky Scientist

Oh no, I didn't know that some food dyes are made from insect shells and that some artificial flavors are made from beaver glandular secretions. I bet some asshole was trying to hide it for nefarious reasons. What's that? They totally had to go through a public and scientific process to get it approved by the FDA. Why wasn't I informed?

Gee whiz, I do sure enjoy this wonderful pain suppressant synthesized from willow bark called aspirin. What's that, most of it's created in a lab now to provide cheap access to millions of people? That's terrible. What's that? It's chemically identical. I don't care, it's obviously different.

I'm glad we have such huge supplies of relatively cheap insulin for all those people with diabetes and related problems. What's that? The majority of insulin is manufactured via GM bacteria. Well shit, it will probably be better for those people to die or pay a lot more money to stay alive just so I feel a little more comfortable with something that I don't understand.

If only there was some way I could avoid eating GM food. You know, other than voluntary GM labels, organic food labels, guarantees by select stores who cater to a clientele such as myself, and numerous apps that can tell me if any processed food product is likely to contain GM. But that all sounds like me doing work so instead I'm going to demand that everybody pay a little more when they buy food. Maybe we should also require people to label food if it has gluten in it or if it's not vegetarian. After all, in my opinion these are healthier alternatives and there's no way that these products will be available to the public without government regulatory requirements.

God those giant corporations sure are evil. They're manipulating people all the time and those poor sods don't even know it. I can't believe they're doing so many terrible things just to make a little money. I'm so glad that I only shop at environmentally and socially conscious companies who would totally never manipulate me just to get me to pay more for something. Boy-o-boy, buying these types of products sure gives me a warm and fuzzy feeling inside.

Sure the majority of science says something is safe, but I'm still a little uncomfortable with some things. What about DDT and some other examples I can come up with where things went wrong? It's just like how I never go out on balconies because I once heard of one that collapsed and killed some people. Never mind that examples of scientific advancements that people were once afraid would cause harm but never did far outweigh those that science told us would be safe but turned out not to be. I bet they weren't that important anyways. I don't really need electricity, anything to do with radio waves, vaccinations, the internet, stem cells, etc, etc.

Oh well, screw broad based scientific proof. I once read something in a blog, or maybe I saw it in a documentary. I can't remember. Besides, this has nothing to do with my subconscious human need to feel superior in some way compared to others. Everyone else is just a bunch of sheep. I'm glad I'm smarter than that. I wish I could have more discussions with knowledgeable people on this subject. Of course by knowledgeable I mean people who have come to the exact same conclusions that I have. Hey, have you read this one study I found that was in this little known scientific journal? Great stuff. No, no I would not like to read your two thousand plus studies. I don't agree with them, so therefore they do not matter. Yes, I do realize that without proof I'm pretty much basing my opinion entirely on faith. What's that? No, no I don't see how this makes this similar to a religious movement.

I don't think I like your tone. You're not acting in a respectable way or valuing my opinion. What do you mean my opinion has no scientific basis? I don't have to put up with this. There's plenty of people I can talk to that agree with me. You just wait, I'll get proven right in the end, you'll see. Then you'll feel really dumb. What do you mean no you won't? What do you mean you'll gladly change your opinions as soon as the data suggests you should? I don't think you realize how important this is. I'm not going to put up with this anymore. I'll say have a nice day, but really I hope you drop dead.

# Forgive Me Father For You Have Sinned

"It's your shot."

"Oh, sorry. What am I again?"

"Stripes."

"Right."

"You want another beer?"

"I don't know. Are you going to have one?"

"I will if you will."

"Don't know if I should. I have to get up early tomorrow. Diane wants to take the kids to church."

"Nice shot."

"Thanks. What the hell, I'll have another beer."

"You're still going to church?"

"Shit, rimmed it. Yeah, Diane wants the kids to have some kind of religion. I'm just along for the ride. Don't you ever go anymore?"

"Nope, haven't been in years."

"I noticed how you never go when we're all back at Mom's."

"Yep."

"She wants you to go you know."

"I know."

"You know it has nothing to do with saving your soul or anything. She just wants to be there with her family."

"I know."

"Couldn't you just go?"

"No."

"That was a close one. Why not?"

"I haven't gone since everything came out about all that altar boy shit."

"Well.....crap......I guess that's pretty understandable. Are we counting slop?"

"Yeah. Go ahead and shoot again. I don't know. It just all seems so fucked up. I guess anymore I'm just a little jaded on the whole organized religion thing."

"Yeah, it's all pretty fucked up. Who knows. Maybe this new Pope can fix things up."

"Maybe. I heard that's it's a big part of why the last one resigned. They needed someone new to clean house."

"Maybe."

"The news said there was some big investigative report that the old Pope left with instructions that it was for the new Pope's eyes only."

"Who knows. Hopefully something happens."

"Yeah."

"Nice shot."

"Thanks."

"It has to be hard for those priests, you know, never getting laid and all."

"I guess."

"I mean hell. Just imagine. Sitting in that damn confessional all day. Listening to people talk about all the deviances you can never do."

"Forgive me father for I have been doing butt stuff with my Mormon girlfriend to save her virginity for marriage. Poor priest is just sitting in that tiny room sweating like a bastard going, uh huh, uh huh, go on my son. Don't spare the details. God needs to know all your transgressions. Fingers desperately working those rosary beads. It's gotta be tough on a person."

"You bet your ass it would be. Tough luck."

"Frickin three ball. You can't see what's going on in that other little room. Sick bastards probably over there choking himself with his god damn rosary and you're just sitting there listening and wondering why it sounds like the priest keeps flipping through his bible so quick."

"Jesus man. Maybe you do need to go to confession."

"Not likely. Shit."

"Tough luck."

"Yeah. Probably over chalked the stick."

"Riiiggghhttt."

"What I don't understand is why it's always altar boys? Why don't they just go out and get themselves a hooker?"

"Availability I guess. There's only so much missionary work that needs to be done down on 82nd street."

"Yeah. I imagine there's a higher likelihood of getting caught with hookers too."

"Sure, can't you just see a group of parishioners walking in on their priest getting a hummer. No, no, you good people misunderstand. This woman is just praying."

"I'm just trying to get the demons out of her. I'm fucking this hooker for Jesus."

"It's your shot."

"Sorry."

"Shit."

"Tough luck."

"Shut up with that."

"Sorry. So what do you think they should do? Let priests marry?"

"I don't know. Maybe they could come up with some kind of compromise."

"Like what?"

"Maybe they could just let priests have sex one day out of the year."

"One day to let their hair down and go crazy."

"Exactly."

"That actually isn't a bad idea. Check out this bank shot."

"It could be right after Easter Sunday. They could call it Misanthropist Monday."

"Malefactor Monday."

"Nice."

"Thank you. Fuck."

"You just can't get that ten ball, can you?"

"You keep distracting me. I got this image in my head of all these priests lying around drinking communion wine and making ribald jokes at each other."

"Ha."

"I bet that it would make Easter mass go really quick too."

"Hell yeah, the priests would be rushing through the readings so they could run down to 82nd street before all the good hookers got taken."

"82nd? Don't you think they'd go for a little more class? You know, like Vegas or something?"

"C'mon, get real. I've got a full year's worth of backed up sexuality pent up and I'm really going to waste a few hours taking a plane ride to a place where slightly better looking hookers have a slightly lower chance of giving me herpes. Christ. Try to be realistic."

"I don't see why it has to be hookers."

"What else are they going to do? Start taking women out on dates a few months before. They have one day a year to get their freak on. They're not going to waste it fucking around."

"Nice pun jackass."

"It happens."

"Fuck that god damn ten ball. How'd I miss that?"

"Beats the fuck out of me. Besides, only hookers are guaranteed to be willing to do all the real kinky shit priests are probably into."

"That's funny. I've always imagined most priests are probably masochists."

"Me too. Sick bastards."

"I imagine that kind of stuff costs extra.

"Sure. Imagined."

"Where are they getting the money for all this anyways? Out of the tithing basket?"

"I guess so."

"Everyone tithe extra this week. Father O'Malley really wants to try a rusty trombone this year. Hey, which one of these is your beer?"

"Just try them both."

"No."

"Just take the fuller one then."

"I don't want to drink out of your beer."

"Why the hell not?"

"I just want to drink my beer."

"Christ, this again. I thought you got past this."

"I guess not."

"We've known each other for years."

"Yeah, but that doesn't mean I know where your mouth has been."

"This is just like that time when you forgot your toothbrush and wouldn't use your wife's."

"I don't see what that has to do with anything."

"God damn it, you kiss her all the time and your mouths have probably been on much filthier parts of each others' bodies."

"It's different."

"How?"

"It just is."

"Jesus."

"......"

"......"

"......"

"Sorry. I think this one is your beer."

"Thanks. You sure?"

"Yeah. Pretty sure. It's your shot."

"Okay. Shit. Looks like I gave you a freebie."

"Thanks."

"Don't worry about it. What about nuns?"

"What?"

"What about nuns? Do they get to celebrate Malefactor Monday too?"

"I don't see why not."

"It only seems fair."

"God, I just got this image in my head of a nun all dressed up in a black leather habit, holding a riding crop and a ball gag."

"Brings a whole new meaning to the term Mother Superior."

"Nice. It would probably solve the hooker issue too."

"Hmmm?"

"Yeah. They could have some kind of key party."

"What, like a bunch of swingers?"

"Exactly. All the priests could put their rosaries into the tabernacle and have the nuns close their eyes and pick them out."

"Seems fair."

"Who's the lucky father who owns this big wooden one?"

"Father O'Malley you lucky bastard. You got Sister Cinnamon. She used to be a stripper."

"Oh sorry Father Henderson, looks like you got Sister Rosemary. She's getting pretty close to seeing the lord personally if you know what I mean."

"Eight ball corner pocket."

"I hope I get Sister Bernadette. She's into butt stuff."

"That's the second time you've mentioned butt stuff."

"Yeah, I get stuck on things sometimes. Usually lasts for a few days."

"Shit."

"And down goes the cue ball."

"You win."

"Technically. You want another beer?"

"Not really. I should probably think about heading home."

"Yeah, we've probably solved as many of the world's problems as we're going to tonight anyways."

"I got to close my tab."

"I'm going to head out."

"See you around."

"Yep."

# The Letter

Dear Helen,

It must seem strange for someone to contact you after nothing but silence for over a year. I know I would find it strange. I have a good life, good friends, good times, adventures, and more smiles than frowns. But we all have something we regret. Something that if we could turn back time, we would try and fix. It's strange. How sometimes someone will say something, or I'll see something, or I'll just be letting my mind wander, and I'll remember. All of it comes flooding back. It's strange. Some of the things that relate to you are some of my greatest regrets, but some others are a great source of pride.

I did the things I did because I cared. I can remember many things, some of which I sometimes wish that I couldn't. I remember seeing the worst your anxiety could dish out. I remember once holding you while you physically shook in my arms, nearly crying. Your eyes filled with fear, sadness, and pain. I remember you asking why was this happening to you. I remember watching you tear yourself apart, bit by bit. I remember being filled with fear and frustration, nothing I could do, nothing I could say, not understanding what was happening. Things like that stick with a person.

I cared because you are one of the most amazing and wonderful people I have ever met. You are smart, witty, driven, and kind. Most of all you are a good person. That is the best term that I can come up with for it. Most of us go through life thinking only of ourselves. Our own wants, our own needs. You put others before yourself. Like the rest of us you aren't perfect, but your heart is always in the right place. I cared because you are somebody who made me feel like I could do better. I cared because you are the type of person who deserves to be cared for.

I learned as much as I could. I did it because I wanted to understand, because I didn't want you to have things like that in your life. It took a long time. I had nobody to talk to about it. By the time I began to put things together you didn't want to talk about it with me anymore. I tried to talk with others, but how do you explain something you don't understand yourself? I read narratives by people who had GAD and people who cared about them. Thousands, there were literally thousands of them. More than anybody could read. I didn't want to just read about others' experiences. I wanted to find a solution. I read scientific papers and articles. I read books and therapy manuals. I learned. I learned everything that I could.

This is the essence of what I learned. Inside of our brains is a small almond sized nuclei called the amygdala which controls emotional reactions. It's in essence the control valve of anxiety. Some people are genetically predisposed to feel more anxiety than others. They're born with a sticky valve. When these people face a problem or worry about something their brain over reacts with more anxiety than normal. This explosion of anxiety results in more worries which in turn results in more anxiety in a vicious self propagating cycle. They begin worrying and experiencing anxiety over the fact that they're experiencing anxiety and can't figure out why. Over time this increased anxiety creates an intolerance of uncertainty, the person seeks to reduce and avoid uncertainty in their lives in order to avoid worrying and the resulting anxiety. Sometimes the person is intolerant to uncertainty in a broad area of things, sometimes only to very specific things. This avoidance reinforces the anxiety response, making it stronger over time. People avoid not only the things that cause them anxiety, but even talking about their anxiety. The brain adapts to this and it becomes normal to the point that the person with GAD is not always aware that they are doing it. The only way out is for the person to stop avoiding their anxiety and to build a tolerance to uncertainty.

I knew that you didn't want to talk about it. I knew you wanted me to forget and move on with my life. But I saw a friend with a problem, a problem they were actively making worse with how they dealt with it. Every time I saw you shaking like a small dog, your own description for it, I felt like I had to do something. How could I sit by and knowingly watch a friend actively hurt themselves? I couldn't do it. Nobody asked me to. You sure as hell didn't want me to. But to me it was the right thing to do.

I hated doing it. I probably hated doing it just as much as you hated me doing it. I had to force myself. I had to force my way through a wall of my own worry, self-doubt, and anxiety. I worried that every time I did it would be the time you got fed up enough to kick me out of your life. I didn't want that to happen. I was all alone, at the time I felt I could not talk to anybody about it. At the time I felt like nobody would understand. I was terrible at it. I could put everything together so well in my head, but when I tried to say it out loud I would just babble. Each time I did it I'd watch you retreat into yourself, stop listening, your mind go somewhere else. I hated it. I always felt like I was talking at you, not to you. Once when I saw you retreat into yourself I purposefully started saying nonsense words. You never noticed. I felt like I couldn't talk to you about anything personal, anything unpleasant. I felt like you expected me to pretend that all the things I'd seen hadn't happened.

I fucked up, a lot. My own worry and anxiety got out of hand. This was something at the time I felt like I couldn't talk about. I tried to hide my own anxiety, from you, those around me, and myself. My anxiety did not help the situation. An inability to deal with uncertainty, that's what my problem boiled down to. When I learned something new I felt like I had to talk to you about it as soon as possible, whether you were ready or not, whether it was a good time for you or not. I needed you to instantly recognize the problem and start doing something about it. I'd get easily frustrated. The frustration would build up and cause me to lose my temper at things, to get mad. All together I ended up probably doing everything the worst way I possibly could for what I was trying to accomplish. It grew and grew until the big blow up after Savannah.

It's an interesting thing about reading and learning about these things. The more I understood the more I was forced to face my own problems. The learning took time. By late spring I really only understood that a lot of people with GAD exhibited similar problems and what the symptoms were. By mid summer I understood the amygdala and how avoidance made anxiety worse. It wasn't until November, after I had lost my shit following Savannah, that I found a book that tied in the intolerance of uncertainty and a strategy of overcoming it using cognitive behavioral therapy. With each step, learning to help you, I was forced to face my own anxiety more and more. I'd flip around from refusing to accept that I had a problem, to avoiding thinking about my problem at all costs, to convincing myself that if I could help you with your problem it would make mine go away. Funny thing about all of these. They only made my anxiety worse. At times I could ignore it, pretend it didn't exist. Other times it floored me, leaving me depressed and feeling hopeless. I hid it from everyone around me. I avoided feeling anything or thinking about it as much as possible.

The big turning point came after the intervention for Denise and the fallout that resulted. It was just one of many bad things that happened around the New Year. The anxiety had spread to all parts of my life. The constant feeling of tension and worry had worn me down. I was scared that everyone could see how badly my anxiety affected me, and it just caused me more anxiety. I got myself put on antidepressants for a while to help myself cope. I re-read the book I had about GAD. It was hard to do, I had panic attacks the entire time while I was doing it, like my anxiety was trying to protect itself. I had to force myself to read it completely through. It was very hard to admit I had a problem. I took some tests in the book, tests meant to see whether or not you have GAD. Each one pointed to me having a problem, I already knew it, I just had to get myself to admit it, one of the harder things I've ever done. At first I told myself I could take care of it on my own. I started keeping a journal of my anxiety attacks, how severe they were, and what I was thinking about when I had them. Finally in mid-January I admitted to myself that it was more than I could handle. I went to see a therapist. It was time to quit making excuses, it was time to quit denying I had a problem, it was time to take responsibility for my own anxiety.

I knew from my research that GAD is often missed by therapists. Many people with it go to 5 or 6 different therapists before they're correctly diagnosed. Often times therapists only notice and try to treat a single symptom without noticing the wider problem. I didn't want to go through that. I specifically picked a therapist that specialized in GAD. When I went into my first appointment I didn't let them tell me what my problem was. Instead I told them what I thought I had, why I thought I had it, and then showed them the book I'd read, the tests I took, and the journal of my anxiety attacks. The therapist agreed with my personal assessment.

At first we just continued doing what I had already started on my own. Keeping track of my anxiety attacks, looking for patterns. It was interesting, 75% of my anxiety was what I called worrying about worrying, or worrying about my anxiety rather than what was causing it. After identifying actual worries we drilled downward rooting out the basis of each of them. I took these worries and applied problem solving techniques. For each one I wrote down options I could take and the different pros and cons for each and then used the information to find solutions. I set goals for myself, things my anxiety was stopping me from doing. I forced myself into situations where I would feel anxiety. It was one of the hardest things I ever had to do.

Years of avoiding my anxiety had made it strong. Just acknowledging my anxiety and talking to somebody about it caused me to have anxiety attacks. But I knew if I didn't talk about it, then I couldn't do anything about it. One of my proudest moments was when my boss asked me why I was taking so many doctor appointments. I told him I was being treated for anxiety. For a while it got worse, not better. Dealing with it was much harder than avoiding it. Sometimes the anxiety attacks were so long, and so bad, that I thought I was going insane. It seemed like I was anxious all the time, my body physically hurt from the constant tension. But the more I forced myself to face my anxiety, the more I forced myself to do the things my anxiety told me not to, the easier it got. I couldn't have started down that path without the therapist. My therapist gave me strategies and direction, and pushed me forward when I wanted to give up. The one thing my therapist couldn't provide, was the motivation for me to help myself.

I'd like to say that I don't have anxiety anymore. But that's not true. I'm always going to feel anxiety. The difference is that now I know I shouldn't let my anxiety choose the direction of my life. I still have anxiety attacks, granted fewer than I used to, but still enough to make me want to hide myself away from time to time. When I do, I just remember it's my amygdala, overreacting and playing a trick on me, and that it will recede in time. I remember that every time I don't react to my anxiety, it gets a little easier to ignore. It's an amazing feeling to get through an anxiety attack, and feel elation rather than depression, because I didn't let it get to me. Sometimes I catch myself falling back into old habits, avoiding things because of my anxiety. It's a constant process of two steps forward and one step back. The difference now is that I know that the problems aren't insurmountable. I know that I can beat it if I try. I don't feel like it's hopeless anymore.

I don't know where my anxiety originally came from. It's obvious now that I had it a long time, long before I met you, and that it especially revolved around me having any kind of emotional commitment or close relationships with people, anything that would hurt too much if I lost it. Who knows what the starting event was? Maybe it was something I was born with? It doesn't really matter. I do know that by avoiding it I let it grow until it became bigger than me, a monster I didn't even know was there. As long as I kept avoiding the things that sparked my anxiety I could pretend it didn't exist. I could enjoy all the other parts of my life, even though I felt a longing for the things I avoided. It wasn't until I really wanted those things that the monster made its presence known, and the full extent of the problem presented itself.

My anxiety and I did a lot of shitty things that hurt you. You and your anxiety did some shitty things to me. Sometimes I wonder why you put up with my shit as long as you did. I imagine it was because you cared about me just like I cared about you. I don't regret trying to help you, I take pride in it. I do regret how badly I fucked it up. I do regret trying to force you to listen, ending so many good memories with bad ones. I do regret letting my anxiety get the better of me time and time again. All the things I did that hurt you number amongst my deepest regrets. I wish I could go back and fix them. But I guess that's life.

Anyways, I really don't expect this to fix anything. I don't expect you to suddenly open up and want to start talking to me again, or start talking about your anxiety. It was wrong of me to try and force you to talk about your anxiety as much as I did. I do miss talking to you and hanging out with you. I can't blame you for kicking me out of your life. I don't expect you to welcome me back into it. These are just some things that I've wanted to get off my chest. Things I've been scared to say for a long time. Well, this email is already too long as it is. Thank you for reading it.

Sincerely,
Your Friend

# Bear Rug

I recently learned that if you want to get a bear rug made it's going to cost you around $6,000 and take as long as a year and half. This might seem like a lot of time and money, but you need to be realistic about the situation. I don't imagine there's that many bear rug makers left in the world. Not just anyone can make bear rugs. It takes a lot of skill to turn a bear carcass into something that anyone trying to turn their living room into a high end 1970's pornographic film set would be proud to have grace their hardwood floor. You know the kind of movie I'm talking about. The kind that actually tries to have a plot and stars people with ridiculous names like Charlie Buttermilk and Chesty McTitterson. Don't pretend you don't know what I'm talking about.

This begs the question, how do people even become a bear rug maker? I never saw that booth at my high school's career day. Maybe its some kind of apprenticeship. I don't know. Bear rug maker doesn't really seem like the kind of career most people set out to get. It's probably something you just kind of fall into.

One day you're stocking groceries onto shelves. You help some random guy find the canned peaches. The two of you strike up a conversation. Next thing you know.......bam........you're an apprentice bear rug maker, on the road to a lifetime of badassery.

That's right. Badassery. Don't try to fool yourself. Bear rug maker is probably the most badass job in the world. I know you think your work in accounting is pretty interesting, but news flash, no one cares. The only job that probably comes close to being as bad ass as bear rug maker is being the personal lion tamer for President Theodore Roosevelt. However, Teddy's been dead for some time now and is giving no signs of coming back, so bear rug maker wins by default. Wait a minute you're probably saying, what about firemen, they're pretty bad ass, and the ladies love them. Please, I don't care if you're a fireman with an accent. There is no way you're pulling more tail than a bear rug maker.

Ladies, imagine you're on a date and you ask the ruggedly macho man across the table from you what he does for a living. He answers that he makes bear rugs. Boom, that's all she wrote. You won't even get through the appetizer before you're telling him it's time to go back to his place for some hot loving making on a massive pile of bear rugs. You'll probably have half your clothes off before you even get out of the restaurant. Some of you will undoubtedly claim that you have too much class and self-respect to ever lose control like that, but that would make you a filthy liar. No woman can resist the masculine charms of a bear rug maker.

Maybe that's why it takes so long to get a bear rug made. Bear rug makers are probably getting so much ass that they only have time to work on bear rugs two hours a day.....tops. Why do you think people buy bear rugs? They do it in the hope that the essence of the bear rug maker will release enough pheromones in their house to jump start their sad little sex lives. It's a verifiable fact that bear rug maker is the number one role-playing fantasy for couples trying to reignite the fire in their relationship. It even beats out classics like Fireman Rescue, Boss and Secretary Working Late, Getting Out of a Speeding Ticket, and Pope John XXIII Missing Easter Mass Because of a Naughty Nun.

If all this has you intrigued and you're thinking about getting a bear rug made, here's a few tips:

1. Make sure you hunt and kill your own bear. Bear rugs require rugged manliness from start to finish. Don't bring a bear rug maker some random bear carcass you found alongside the highway.

2. Don't send your wife or girlfriend to drop off your bear carcass or pick up your bear rug when it's done. I don't care how faithful they are, once they walk through the door of the bear rug maker's shop they're going to be hit by so much raging machismo that it's going to reduce them to the state of a teenager at a pop concert.

3. It's legal to mail your bear carcass to the bear rug maker. Sure the box might be heavy, drip a little blood, and definitely stink up the mail truck, but screw the mailman, he's union and gets four weeks of vacation a year.

4. Don't wear your bear rug like a robe and walk around your house talking in a racist Native American accent or making poor quality bear sounds. Bear rugs are supposed to be classy. Let's keep them that way.

This is totally not brought to you by the North American Bear Rug Association based in Saskatoon, Saskatchewan. I was in no way paid fat wads of colorful monopoly like Canadian dollars to write this.

# Grammie

The room is small. Just enough space for a small kitchenette, a couch, a television, and a cramped desk. A door leads off to a humble bedroom and bathroom. A machine in the corner constantly hums. A clear tube snakes across the room to the old woman sitting on the couch. Holes in the hose constantly blow oxygen into her nose with a soft hiss. The old woman has gray hair that was once black. The skin on her hands appears shiny, as though it is thin and over polished. Here and there small bruises leave dark stains in places on her arms. She bruises easily now. She is old, far older than I remember her.

The old woman watches with interest as I sit on the floor and fiddle with computer wires that, when I'm done, will connect the tower, screen, keyboard, and mouse into a single unit. The old woman's voice sounds roughened when she speaks.

"Are you sure you got all of the right wires?"

"Yes. I made double sure before I drove down from the house."

"Thank you very much for doing this."

"No problem."

The old woman lets out a deep hacking phlegmy cough. It's the kind of cough where you wonder if a lung is going to come up. I keep my eyes on my work, but inside I feel a deep sense of unease, worry, and physical disgust. It is a disgusting cough to hear, one that makes you feel a strong agitation in your own throat in sympathy. I feel immediate shame for my disgust. One could say that it wasn't her fault that she had such coughs, but that wouldn't be the truth. My grandmother quit smoking when I was nine. At least those were the last memories I had of her driving us to her house, window slightly open, cigarette held up by the window to keep the smoke out of the car. We all have vices. We all have things we can't give up. She was always careful. I never saw her smoke after she told us she quit, but quitting was just an illusion, just a banishment of the vice into the shadows.

There is silence after the coughing fit ends. I have been here most of the morning, visiting my Grammie, the title by which we had always called her. A word that had brought me excitement from the time I was very small. It had been a nice day. My grandmother had me load an oxygen tank onto her cart and she gave me a tour of the building. She smiled happily and showed off her grandson to her fellow prisoners of aging bodies. She made jokes and whispered gossip about the various people that we ran into.

"That's so and so. He's not really all here anymore." I smile politely. "I can't remember her name. I feel bad for her. Nobody ever comes to visit her."

She smiles and jokes the entire time, but I can tell that she doesn't want to be here. Her brick house up on the hill overlooking the small town is less than a mile away. The house with the big windows that she always wanted my brothers and me to play football near, in hopes that she could have an excuse to replace them. The house that we drove to every year for

Christmas to open a second round of presents. The house where we did our easter egg hunts, my uncle always hiding one up in the gutter so that we wouldn't be able to find it. She didn't want to move down here. She didn't want to leave her house, but I guess we don't always get what we want.

After the tour we go back to her room, and after helping her rehook her hose to the machine in the corner, we talk about whatever comes to our minds. She asks about school and I tell her I'm doing fine. I tell her about the classes I'm taking and the various things that I've learned. She has me get a Pepsi from the room's mini fridge and makes me wash off the top in the sink before I drink it. We sit and talk for hours. Sometimes the conversation hits a lull and we're quiet for a little while. Neither one of us seems to mind. I've never felt uncomfortable around my grandmother.

A nurse comes in for a short while. She smiles a lot and talks in an even calm voice. After introductions and some small talk, I politely stare at some pictures on the wall, studying every detail and pretending not to listen as my grandmother gets put through a barrage of questions on how she's feeling today and then is given a quick physical. Blood pressure, heart beat, listening to her lungs. The nurse leaves and we are alone once again.

She never pries, but yet I always try to find more things to tell her about. There is something in the silence, something that lets me know it will be okay to talk about anything. I tell her about some of the people in the fraternity I'm in, some of them that I don't like. She listens and plays devil's advocate. Forcing me to think about others points of view. I tell her about some of my worries and some of my concerns. She listens, interrupting only to make comforting comments. When I seem to get too down she tells me a story about something funny or interesting. Something to take my mind off of the troubles of the world. When she does, I try to change my own stories to be more light hearted as well. My grandmother is a wonderful woman. I've never felt out of place around my grandmother. I've always felt like she understood me, that I didn't have to try to explain myself to her, what made me tick. There is nobody else that I can say this about.

As I work on the computer I look up at the side table where the other item that I got from her house sits. Just like the computer she was very specific about me bringing it down. It's a rarely read bible, encased in old, but unworn, black leather. I know that officially my grandmother is a Methodist, but I have never once seen her go to church on Sunday, read the bible, or even really ever talk about God. It is just one more sign of the inevitable. Just one more item that when taken into conjunction with her cart, the hissing machine in the corner, and the room itself, give proof to a truth that I banish from my head whenever it makes its way to the front of the queue. Time is short.

I get done with the computer and make sure everything boots up without problems. My grandmother smiles.

"Thank you very much. It's so nice to have my computer again."

My grandmother has always enjoyed technology. Hers was the first house where I saw a VCR, polaroid camera, fax machine, home copier, and modern personal computer with a Windows operating system. She enjoys electronic stores the same way stereotypical women enjoy clothing stores. She could walk through them for hours, keenly picking through all the advancements in the world of home office equipment.

I have to go. I'm heading back up to college tomorrow and it's a five hour drive. It will probably be even longer because of the snow. I walk over to the couch where she sits and give her a hug. She squeezes back. I pretend not to notice that her hug is not as strong as it once was. I pull back and sit next to her for a second. She reaches out and gives my hand a squeeze. Her eyes sparkle for a moment like they use to.

"Thank you again for the computer. It was very nice of you to get it for me."

"It was no problem. I was glad to do it."

"I'm glad that you came. You're the only one who still treats me like a person."

I squeeze her hand back. It's an unfair statement. It's easy for me. I don't have to come by on a regular basis and watch her slowly drift away. I can go back to college and pretend that nothing is going to change. That the world of my childhood will always be there when I make the drive back home.

"I'm always glad to help." We hug again and I get up and put on my coat. "I'll visit you next time I'm back in town."

"I'll look forward to it."

"Me too."

I turn and walk out the door.

It is a lie. A few words my mother told me as I left the house that morning hang in my mind. My grandmother and I both know that it is a lie, but yet we still give these pleasantries, trying to provide comfort to each other. I try not to dwell on it as I drive away.

It's only a month later that I return home from college to attend my grandmother's funeral. I stand in an old sports coat, once owned by a long dead great uncle, amongst my family at the church. The casket sits before us, but the entire thing seems unreal. I listen to the nice words, the eulogy, ride in a slowly moving car, and then watch my grandmother's casket get set on a metal stand over its grave. I do not cry during the service. I do not cry at the graveside. I do not cry at the reception. I am a stone. I feel nothing. I hug and comfort my mother several of the numerous times she breaks down, but I do not feel a part of the moment. I feel like I am a spectator watching the world around me.

After all is done we get in the family car and drive home. I get into more comfortable clothes and stay up for a little while reading. I then brush my teeth and go to bed. The house is silent, everyone else has already long ago fallen asleep. I lay in my bed and my mind plays a film, all that I can remember. The rock cracks and it comes flooding in. She's gone. She's gone. She's forever gone. Tears fill my eyes and overflow down my cheeks. I sob quietly. Alone.

# Poison

It is a beautiful day in early summer. A light breeze blows down the river canyon where we hike. Myself, Pabst, Steve, Eric, and my two brothers all carry light packs. It is only a day hike. The sun shines downward, but we only sweat lightly. The river is small, but swift. The canyon is steep and dotted with basalt outcroppings, sagebrush, and juniper trees. It is an environ that is pleasing to my eyes, the environ I was born in. The sights, sounds, and smells are all of home.

We come upon a small pine glade along the edge of the river. Inside it is shaded, hidden from the outside world. Each step crunches downward through years of fallen needles, a soft carpet of tiny daggers which muffle all sounds as we move through it. Dust motes float on shafts of light which have broken through the branches from the sky above. Small pixies lazily flying in the warm summer air. It is a strange place, a stifling place. We all get quiet as we walk through it. The glade has the same feeling as a church, the feeling that one must be silent and respectful while one is within.

In the center of the pine glade we find an old picnic table, its paint peeled off in great strips. Wisps of sunlight from above create patches of light around it. On top lays the remains of a long abandoned picnic. An old falling apart wicker basket, a large aged rusty thermos, old metal plates and utensils which have been picked clean by insects, rotted paper wrappings, and what appears to be the remains of a watermelon which has collapsed in on itself. All is covered in dust, mold, and mildew. It is a strange scene to behold. You can almost hear the happy laughter of the bygone gathering which was once held here.

Strangest of all is the large wooden cup set near the middle. The cup is nearly a foot high and carved into the shape of a grinning tiki mask. It is filled to the brim with water, the slow accumulation of rain falling through the trees. Unlike everything else on the table the cup is not covered in dust or cobwebs, it appears clean and new as though it was just set there the day before.

I don't know what strange sensation and need comes over me. I reach forward and flick the top of the tiki cup with my finger. A few droplets of water slop over the side and fall, splashing on the dusty tabletop. A shape lashes forward, knocking pieces of forgotten picnic out of its way. I feel a sudden sting on my wrist. All of us jump away from the table as the shape coils back, hissing, ready to strike again. Two snakes writhe against each other in the center of the table, their bodies coiling and uncoiling, making it difficult to tell where one snake ends and the other begins. Their dry scaly skin rustles as they rub against one another. They hiss in anger, both at each other and at the intruders to the glade. Both snakes have their tails jammed into the same knothole on the table, trapping them together in a permanent embrace.

I stare at the snakes intently, trying to make out their colors and markings in the dim light. My heart is pounding. Please god no. Flashes of white belly and then the dark brown and the gray of their tops. Patterns of diamonds spread downward across their backs. Rattlesnakes! The certainty drives a deep fear into me. I take a few deep breaths and try to get my heart to slow its heavy rhythm. I look at my wrist and see the small gash near the blue veins that track just below the surface. It does not appear to be a bad bite, but there is no reason to take the chance.

"We have to go." The others look from the snakes to me, shock and puzzlement in their eye. "We have to go. I've been bitten."

One by one the bulbs light over their heads and the reasoning behind my words sink in. Steve is the first to talk. "Are you going to be okay?"

"Yeah, it's really just a scratch. But we should probably get it checked out."

My older brother turns and starts walking. "Let's go then. The car isn't that far."

We leave the glade and hike another half mile down the canyon. I try to keep my breathing deep, long, and even. Try to keep my heart from beating too fast. My brothers and friends give me shit the entire walk. Trying to make me mad. Their words do nothing, but the fact that they're trying to make me have a strong reaction at the one time I need to remain completely calm makes me angry. Why are they being such assholes? I suppress and ignore it. I tell myself to remain serene, to not let them get to me. I do my best. I look down at the gash again. It's not bad. It isn't even swelling. So why do I still feel so worried?

We reach the car and get in, my older brother behind the steering wheel. We pull out of the parking lot and start the drive home. My eyes watch the passing landscape and my mind wanders. Who put the tiki cup in the glade? How did the snakes get their tails caught in the knothole? What is going on?

The change is abrupt, like the flipping of a television channel. One second I'm in the car, the next I'm in a

Shakespearean throne room. Torches and lamps flicker along the walls. Lords, ladies, jesters, soldiers, and peasants all wait for their chance to talk to the fat king who sits on the throne in the center. His face is jowly and pale beneath a wispy beard. His bulging shoulders are covered in soft furs. Gold chains hang around his neck. His great belly bulges out against his tunic, hiding his lap and codpiece beneath its fold. His plump fingers are covered in rings. His legs, encased in tights, are skinny and bony, in sharp contrast with the rest of him. The fat king stares out at the world through pig like eyes. He cannot see me. I can feel that I am not physically there. It is just a vision.

Two assassins come forward and give their report to the king. They tell him how they have slain the hero that was the king's nemesis and that the hero will never challenge the king's authority again. The king chortles and laughs at the news, his great belly shaking, and then demands to know how the deed was done. The assassins hand the king a golden chalice and then begin a soliloquy about poison and how cleverly they got the hero to consume it. The fat king sits and listens and raises the cup to his lips to take a drink.

The assassins and the entire court fall into a shocked silence. The fat stupid king demands to know what is wrong. Nobody can find the words to answer him. The king's neck begins to convulse and he looks confused. He puts the chalice down and stands up and begins walking back and forth. He stops and raises his hand, tries to speak, but nothing comes out. The entire court watches in stunned disbelief. No one tries to raise a finger to help the fat stupid king who can't figure out what is happening. He tries one last time to speak, and then drops over dead.

Another abrupt change. I am back in the car and we are pulling up at my parents' house. None of it is real. I shake my head and concentrate on the task at hand. We have to hurry, the nearest clinic is still half an hour drive away. We get out of the car and rush to tell my parents what has happened. The house is crowded, my parents' entire network of extended family and friends in one place to have a celebration. There is a momentary point of panic. My wrist still has not swelled and I feel foolish for causing such a ruckus over nothing. I feel eerily calm, wishing that we could just get done with it already so I could continue with my day. Nothing is going to happen, it will just be an interesting story to tell people later.

There is a momentary time of confusion as people debate on who should accompany me to see the doctor. A group of us slip out as the debate continues. We don't have time for this. We all get into my parent's SUV. Me, my mom, Eric, my dad's cousin's wife, and Pabst behind the wheel. He turns on the engine and mashes the accelerator to the floor, throwing gravel as he pulls out of the driveway. I look at my wrist again, the small gash barely breaking the skin. I don't feel entirely connected to the moment. I don't feel like I'm entirely there.

When I look up again I do not see the rural setting of my boyhood home. I see the SUV darting in and out of traffic, passing cars on both the left and right as it moves down the expressway in a heavily urban setting. Tall buildings blot out large parts of the sky. Roadways and exits surround us on all sides. Pabst misses the exit he wanted to take. It moves below us, separated by a downward sloping cement embankment. There is no time to wait, no time to try again. "Hang on," I hear Pabst yell, and then he jerks the wheel, sending the SUV down over the side. Cars honk their horns and angry faces appear in all the surrounding windshields, but with another jerk of the wheel we are right where we need to be, speeding down the exit to the hospital.

There is a bridge ahead, a bridge with no river below it. Crossing guards close and the bridge begins to slowly rise in front of us. Pabst guns the engine of the SUV and crashes through the crossing guard. Pabst has his foot to the floor, the pedal to the metal. The SUV moves farther and farther up an ever steepening incline. I wrestle to get on my seatbelt. Everyone in the car is screaming except for me. My heart is pounding, but I am silent. I do not feel like I am actually there. I am unafraid. I know that nothing bad is going to happen. My heart is at first beating rapidly, but it slows as I become less of an actor in the play around me, and more of a spectator.

We are nearly at the top when the bridge hits 90 degrees. The SUV, its wheels still spinning, begins to fall back to the earth below. People continue to scream all around me, but it is all in slow motion. The various random loose items that can be found in all cars hang in the air around me. I watch in captivated interest as we fall, the action unfolding around me at a tenth of normal speed. I feel as though I am weightless, as though I could unhook my seatbelt, open the car door, and float away.

I do not remember the crash. One moment we are hanging in the air. The next we are all piling out of the ruined car and climbing over a railing and a steep embankment to the street below. Nobody seems to be hurt. The moment of unreality ends. I am again part of the action, I am no longer just watching. We don't run, running will just spread the poison, if there is any, through my body faster. We keep up a brisk walk. As we round the first block we hear three gunshots in the distance. My mother looks worried, but the rest of us ignore it and keep moving.

We move onto a sidewalk covered with scaffolding to keep the construction above from falling onto the people below. The sidewalk is crowded, lots of people walking this way and that and small two person tables, all occupied, lining the wall. I walk at a quickened pace, but my footsteps are uneven. I feel like I am drunk, my motor skills slowly going to hell. With each step the feeling becomes stronger. My entire body feels off balance. I keep pressing myself forward.

The sidewalk becomes more crowded and I am forced to push my way through. I don't see any of the people that we're in the SUV with me. More and more people start appearing in baby blue tracksuits. They are all younger black men, wearing white dew rags. My brain instantly snaps in a picture of a gang shooting up the streets. I slow down, not willing to push and antagonize these men. My mind snaps back to the gunshots we heard when we left the car. My eyes fall back onto the wound on my wrist. How long has it been? How long do I have?

I feel as though I am driving my body via remote control from a long distance away. Commands from my brain to my limbs are scattered and unsure. I can feel my worry rising as I lose more and more control of my ability to walk a straight line. Everything moves around me in a blur, the details becoming less succinct and definite. I pass by one of the tables. A small white blonde girl with glasses sits at it in the same baby blue track suit as the gang bangers. I overhear her explain to somebody that their church group is here to help the poor and clean graffiti, that they are always getting confused for a gang. I don't hear the rest, but I feel a wave of guilt pass over me for my earlier assumptions.

The scaffolding and sidewalk end and the crowds disperse. I feel myself fall forward onto my hands and knees. I am not sure if I fall because I truly lost my balance or if I do it only for dramatic affect, a cry for help to the people around me. I feel someone lift me up, and I turn my head to see my mother. We hustle across the now eerily empty streets, her arm around me helping to support me. I don't feel like I can move forward on my own anymore. I feel worried, but I am still not afraid. Everything will turn out alright.

My mother's voice is quiet and easily swallowed by the empty urban setting around us. "Your father and I have been watching a lot of TV shows online."

"What?"

"You're better now than you were. I didn't think you could get her back before, but now maybe I think you can."

"What?"

My mother keeps looking forward and hustling me on, my clumsy legs barely supporting my own weight. It is as though she didn't say anything at all. I feel like I should say something more to break the silence.

"My friend gave me the password for her account. I'll give it to you when we get home. Then you can watch all the shows you want."

My mother looks confused but smiles at me. "That would be nice."

I look up and realize I'm not sure where we are. The streets are empty. Great columns of concrete hold the freeway over our heads.

"Hey idgets, you walked right past it." My mother and I turn and see Eric running down the street to a nearby door behind us. Everyone else from the car is a little ways behind him, hustling to catch up. Our conversation has distracted us. We walked right past the hospital.

We hurry back and walk through the hospital doors. The waiting room is full and busy looking. Everyone stops what they are doing and looks up when we barge in. My mother takes the lead.

"Snakebite. Poison."

Two men in white coats rush forward and throw my arms over their shoulders. They half carry, half drag me through a pair of swinging doors. We go into a room and they lay me onto a cold tiled floor. The room is not a hospital room. It looks like a dispensary. Shelves of bottled medications line the walls. The doctors working on me look like they could be brothers. They both look like the actor Bryan Cranston. One has a full head of hair and looks like the dad from the popular comedy show. One is bald and has a goatee and looks like the science teacher who

makes meth from the popular drama. The people who rode in
the SUV with me all come in and line up out of the way against
the wall. They watch intently but their faces betray no emotion.
Everything feels unreal, as though I'm not really there. It's as
though I've fallen deeper into my body and everything
happening is from a farther distance away. The doctors work
feverishly.

"Check his glands," yells the bald one.

They both even sound like Bryan Cranston.

"Hook up that draining tube," snaps the full head of hair
one.

I raise my wrist to try and show them my wound but they
push my arm back down. The bald one cuts off my right pant
leg with a scalpel and shoves a large needle into my leg above
my knee. Liquid begins to flow through a rubber tube attached
to the needle, out of my field of vision. The one with a full head
of hair keeps popping tiny pills off a sheet of plastic and putting
them in my mouth where they dissolve. They taste bitter. I can
feel my throat start to tighten. It becomes harder to draw in
breaths. My hand tries to grip the arm of the doctor with hair.

The doctor with no hair looks at my mother. "Has he been
hallucinating?"

"Yes."

The two doctors look at each other with mirrored worried
expressions.

The one with hair has a look on his face like he's trying to
solve a rubik's cube. "What about dialysis?"

"Too late."

Breathing becomes harder. Each breath only brings in half
as much air. I can feel gurgling in my lungs with every breath.
Orange colored spittle comes from my mouth with every exhale.
I struggle, trying to breath harder to get enough air. A larger
amount of orange colored liquid comes out of my mouth,
splattering my front and the hand of the doctor with hair who

continues to shove the little pills into my maw. Panic. I shake
his arm in desperation. The doctor with hair leans in close. For
a moment I wonder if he's going to give me mouth to mouth. I
feel myself instinctively recoil away.

"You need to stay calm. We're doing everything we can for
you. You need to stay calm."

I look into his eyes and I know. I know that I'm not going to
live. I'm going to die here on this dispensary floor. My right leg
jerks upward toward the ceiling, liquid continues to flow through
the tube. The bald doctor pushes my leg back down. Breathing
becomes harder and harder. I'm choking, suffocating. I begin to
panic. My arms begin to flail, but the doctor with hair holds
them down. My eyes rove the room and land on my mother. I
try to speak, but I cannot. There is so much I want to say. So
many messages that I wanted to leave if this happened. I was
never meant to die like this.

I am laying in bed at home, warm and safe underneath my
covers. Protectively cocooned by layers of blankets. Not asleep,
but not awake. Mid-morning light brightens the curtains which
cover the window and keep the room in shadows which shift
imperceptibly as the sun heaves its way across the sky. I see
none of these things, but I can feel all of them. I'm laying on the
cold dispensary floor. Choking. Desperate. Scared. Watching
those standing around me who can do nothing to help. I can feel
myself slipping away as my supply of oxygen is cut off. I can
feel my brain begin to slow. Each ragged breath helps less and
less. I am in both places at the same time. I am in my bedroom
and on the dispensary floor. It's a strange and disconcerting
feeling. I am in both worlds, but not entirely part of either. This
is not the way I want to die. I am not dying. There is so much I
still need to say. I still have time to do so. What is happening?
What is going on?

I am trapped. I don't know what to do. I feel comfortable
and safe at the same time as I feel panicky and scared, my mind

slowing shutting down into emptiness. Each ragged gurgling breath becomes harder and harder, bringing in less and less air. I can feel myself lying on my bed, desperately gulping in long deep breaths. They do nothing to help me on the icy cold dispensary floor. My heartbeat is rapid. I can feel my blood in every artery, vein, and capillary. My cells are vibrating in their terror. I stare at my mother through a long tunnel of darkness. The light above her flickers. My chest aches and my lungs burn. I feel one last thought, one last popping synapse. I wish.... I wish.... and then nothing. My mind and body lurches. I feel a warm comfort envelope me, shadowy darkness all around me. The feeling of the cold dispensary floor and the sounds of those around me disappear. It's gone. It's all gone.

# Crazy, I Was Crazy Once

What if I am the one who is crazy?  A friend once described for me what it meant to be around someone who is crazy.  You're riding in a car with them and you get to a green light.  It's obvious it is a green light, everyone knows that it is a green light.  Yet your friend stops, to them it's a red light.  You try to tell them to go, but they won't.  No matter how you try to debate and argue they do not see what is obvious to everyone else.  They see a red light.  It seems so simple, so cut and dried, but it's not.

What if you have never talked with anyone about green lights?  What if in your entire life you have avoided the subject of green lights whenever it has come up?  What if the entire subject of what color the light is makes you and everybody around you uncomfortable?  So nobody ever talks about it.  You pull up to the green light, your friend says that it's red.  How can you prove that they're wrong?  How can you prove that your perceptions are not the ones that have been skewed?

Even if you talk to friends about what color the lights are, you never say everything that is on your mind.  What if the parts you held back are the parts that show you are wrong? What if the only reason they agree with you is because you did not tell them the entire story? What if in all the times you discussed stoplights you never once mentioned the colors? What if your friends don't really agree with you but are being nice because they care about you? They don't want to hurt you. What if they perceive that being your friend and letting you see the light as red is better than possibly losing your friendship and forcing you to go through severe psychological trauma as the delusion is pulled asunder?

Imagine yourself as this person. How would you react when one person stands up and tries to tell you the light is green? One person who doesn't want to see you get hurt in an accident caused by constantly stopping at intersections you don't need to stop at. Imagine. Who would you listen to? All your life you have seen the light as red, and no one has ever told you anything different, then one lone crazy person pops up and says that you are wrong. You may have your own doubts. You may notice that you are the only car that is stopping at the intersection. You may watch all the other cars drive through without stopping and wish you could just blow right through too. But the light is red to you, it has always been red to you. Which is easier, to rethink how you perceive reality and examine the cracks in your psyche, or to see the one person who is willing to speak up as a lunatic?

Maybe I am crazy? Either way, it apparently isn't a valid excuse to get out of a ticket for running a red light.

# Ich Bin Fertig

Wilhelm stood on his porch with a snifter half full of brandy in hand. He swayed slightly from side to side as though he was on the deck of a ship, though he had not been on one since he crossed the Atlantic twenty years before. Daniel Gibbs grunted as he carried another heavy load from the back of his truck to the porch. Foodstuffs and other perishables, a few bolts of cloth that Lilith had ordered, a box of medicine for the cows, and several large cans with enough kerosene to last a month. Only a few years ago Daniel would have been carrying the loads from the back of his wagon, but the times were changing. Once Wilhelm would have never stood on his porch while a man worked in front of him, but things were different now.

Daniel finished his task and leaned against the porch railing, hiding in the shade from the hot Texas sun. He took a handkerchief from his back pocket and wiped his sweaty brow.

"Well, that's everything Mr. Kraus. Those phonograph records haven't come in yet, but I'll bring them out as soon as they do."

"Yes, that is fine." Wilhelm had been in America long enough that his own heavy German accent was noticeable in his ears.

Daniel looked down at the large cans of kerosene. "That's a lot of kerosene you got there Mr. Kraus. I know it's none of my business, but I've never delivered so much kerosene at one time before."

"I do not like the dark." Wilhelm tipped back his glass and finished the last of his brandy. He toyed with the empty glass, slowly turning it this way and that. He watched young Daniel's bright blue eyes as they stared at the glass. Daniel took after his mother, but his eyes belonged to his father, Nelson, one of Wilhelm's oldest friends.

Daniel's eyes rose and tracked over the empty barnyard, the corral with its gates all askew, and the few skinny cows munching on bunchgrass on the side of the draw. "Do you need anything before I go Mr. Kraus?"

"Nein, ich brauche nichts." Wilhelm saw the confusion spread across Daniel's face and realized that he had said the words in German instead of English. Wilhelm licked his lips and repeated himself again. "No, I am fine."

The look on Daniel's face did not look like he believed him. But Daniel was a good boy, he had been raised right. Daniel nodded his head. "Alright then. I better be getting back into town. I'll bring those phonographs out when they come in."

Daniel stood facing Wilhelm. The two men stared at each other in silence. Daniel was obviously uncomfortable, but for some reason couldn't leave. Finally understanding sparked across Wilhelm's brain. He reached into his pocket and pulled out a mess of coins and paper bills, shoving them into the boy's hands.

"This should cover it."

The boy eyed the money in his hand. "This is too much Mr. Kraus."

Wilhelm waved his hand absently. "Just put the extra towards the next delivery."

Daniel stood for a moment longer. His face a mask of confusion. But he was a good boy. He had been raised right. "Okay Mr. Kraus. You have yourself a good day."

"You too." The response was automatic. Wilhelm didn't really care. Daniel climbed into his truck and started it. The few skinny cows on the hillside looked up from their grazing at the sudden noise. With a grind of gears, and a squeak of shocks, the truck climbed the side of the draw and headed back out towards the main road. Wilhelm watched until it disappeared out of sight and then turned to go back inside, leaving the delivered goods on the porch.

Once Wilhelm would have taken his wagon into town for his own supplies. But he didn't like going there anymore. Things had changed during the war. The older people who had always known him treated him the same, though some were notably less friendly and gave him wary looks, as though he was a rattlesnake too close to the hen house. The new people, and the young men who came back from the trenches, were more open with their distaste. The word Hun had been heard many times behind his back. Many of his fellow Germans had changed their names, trying to show they wanted to be Americans. Wilhelm had refused. He was stubborn and could not see what his name had to do with his love for his adopted homeland. In Germany he had been a poor workman's son. In America he was a prosperous gentleman.

The house was filled with dust. It was nearly impossible to keep a house clean in the West Texas desert, and the fight had long ago been given up. Wilhelm walked to a table in the corner, covered in an assortment of bottles filled with varying volumes, and poured himself another drink. This one was whiskey. His hands shook when he poured. Once they had been strong and steady, but that had left him along with everything else.

Wilhelm looked up and caught sight of himself in the filthy mirror above the table. Long greasy hair that had once formed a thick comb over now hung limply down one side of his head. His large mustache, once curled on the ends with wax, now hung limp on either side of his sour looking mouth. His shirt was rumpled and stained, with the top two buttons undone. Wilhelm could not look himself in the eye. He was willing to look at everything else, but the eyes had to be avoided. He could not bear to see what they showed.

Wilhelm walked over to the bookshelf, stuffed with classics in both German and English. Most of the English ones belonged to his wife and children, classics by famous American and British authors. Most of the German ones belonged to him. Siegfried and Beowulf. Kings and heroes from a forgotten age. Wilhelm ran his hands over the leather bindings and selected one at random. He took his book and new drink, and sat down in a dark green chair. The chair was well stuffed and comfortable, but it really didn't matter. He took a sip of his drink and opened the book. Wilhelm tried to read for a bit but found his mind kept drifting away from the words on the pages. He stood up and put the book back in its place on the bookshelf.

Wilhelm stared out the window at his life's work baking in the hot sun. The large barn and nearby corrals stood empty. Once they had contained a remuda of thirty-five fine quarter horses. Wilhelm had an eye for horses and people had once claimed they were the finest group of horses in that part of the state. Wilhelm had opened the corral gate and let them out a few weeks ago. They were likely spread across the countryside by now. He had kept forgetting to feed them and thought it better to let them go. Let them have a chance. He had done the same with the pigs and chickens.

Wilhelm took another sip of his drink. Once he had been able to drink enough to make all the numbness go away. Once he could drink enough that all could be forgotten and joy could sweep back in. Over time it had taken more and more to make it happen, and now he usually passed out before he noticed any difference. He'd awaken from his stupor at odd hours, his head full of pain and his heart full of grief, and then he would start again. His stomach growled and for a moment Wilhelm wondered how long it had been since he'd eaten. It didn't really matter.

The stove in the big kitchen had been cold since Lilith had left. Wilhelm could see her jet black hair streaked with gray, her sharp nose, and her high cheekbones. Lilith was a full blooded Indian. He had first met her when he had nothing, working as a ranch hand in Oklahoma back when it was still the Indian Territory. To a young lad from Bavaria she had seemed the most exotic woman in the world. She was so beautiful. When they had first married he still barely spoke any English. They would sit hand in hand and she would teach him how to shape the words.

A month ago she had walked out the door. Wilhelm had awakened himself enough from his stupor to follow her out onto the porch. Her eyes had been wet, red, and puffy. In all the long years of their marriage, Wilhelm had never seen her cry. She had a hard determined look on her face, and had carried a small bag slung over her shoulder.

"Where are you going?" he had asked.

Her dark eyes sat in her dark face, windows to the soul closed off so none could see inside. Her voice had been flat when she had spoken. "I am going away. I am going away to be with my children."

The two had stared at each other in silence. Her eyes had been emotionless, and his had been full of tears. "But what am I supposed to do? What am I supposed to do without you?"

"I do not know. I do not know what you should do. But I want to be with my children. I have to be with my children."

She had turned then and started walking away at a steady pace. Not quick but not slow. Wilhelm had watched her go, and in his grief yelled out her name several times, but she had not turned. The world was already fading into twilight when her slim body had disappeared over the horizon and all was swallowed up by darkness. Wilhelm had thought about giving chase, but he had not. He had known it would do no good. She was a stubborn woman and her mind had been made up. He could chase her down and drag her back. But he knew in the end she would get what she wanted. Instead he had gone back inside and poured himself another drink. For a while he had held out hope that she would come back. That maybe she had changed her mind. After a week he had accepted the new reality. Wilhelm had always been a sensible man.

Wilhelm finished his drink as he stared out at the landscape of the draw. Loose dirt, bunchgrass, and sagebrush. All contained in the little world that he had created so carefully for himself and his family. He thought about pouring himself another, but changed his mind. He had things he needed to do today. Things that had to get done.

Wilhelm put down his glass and took an old hat down from a coat rack next to the front door. It was covered in dirt and no longer held its shape, but it fit his head like it was a part of him. Wilhelm walked outside and filled an old metal bucket with water from a hand pump. The delivered goods still sat where Daniel had left them in neat piles on the porch. Wilhelm carried the full bucket across the yard and behind the barn. The cows on the hillside watched him for a bit and then went back to munching grass.

Wilhelm watched them as he walked. The few cows on the hill were just a small portion of his herd. Fifteen hundred head were scattered across the surrounding rangelands. The work of a lifetime started from five old cows given to him by old Mr. Thompson in lieu of payment one winter near Amarillo when money had been tight for everyone. Those had been tough times, but he and Lilith had been tougher. From those five old bags of bones had sprung one of the finest herds in West Texas. Wilhelm had a good eye for breeding stock. His steers were always fat, his cows were always good mothers, and his bull calves were always in high demand.

The herd was probably more scattered than it should have been, but that was natural given that nobody was watching it. This year's crop of calves should have already been branded by now. Undoubtedly some were, just not with Wilhelm's brand. The hands had not been hired to do the work. The cows had not been rounded up and they had not been trailed to the sweet summer grasses of the hills. It didn't really matter.

One hundred yards behind the barn, where the hill started to rise upwards, a young oak, just ten feet tall, stood. It's green leaves, on upward pointing branches, fluttered at the slightest breeze. Wilhelm had planted the tree with his own hands just a year and a half ago, and watered it with his own tears. Beneath the tree sat three gravestones in a nice straight row. Wildflowers bloomed in three bunches in front of each.

Once there had been a fourth grave, set off slightly by itself. The grave had been smaller and of rougher quality. Wilhelm had torn it down one night in a drunken rage and smashed it with a sledge until only gravel remained. The night had been wet and cold, rain lashing him like a beast, and lighting forking across the sky, but he had refused to come back inside until all evidence of the marker had been destroyed. It was an evil thing, a vile thing, and it did not deserve to be remembered.

A hired hand had been the first to sicken. A man in his mid-twenties named Joe Meeks who helped to watch the herd and care for the horses. He came back from town after taking a weekend off to waste his money on alcohol and women. He had fallen sick soon afterwards. His condition had worsened with a fever, shakes, weakness, sore throat, and sweating. It became so bad that they had moved him into the house from where he normally slept in the barn's hay loft. The doctor had been summoned, but he could do nothing and Joe died soon afterwards. The doctor had said he died of pneumonia. They buried him behind the barn. He had no family in the area.

Wilhelm poured the water from the bucket onto the base of the oak and then sat down by the graves. Wilhelm had known it was not pneumonia. The paper's had been full of stories about the influenza outbreak burning its way across the country. Numerous cases had already been reported in El Paso and other nearby communities by the time Joe died. Wilhelm's ranch was isolated and a long ways from anywhere. It had seemed just like the war, a problem of the far off world that had little to do with the daily life on the ranch.

William, the eldest, had been the first. The big strapping lad of seventeen with his mother's dark skin and somber looks. He was large and strong, and no job ever seemed too much for him. Wilhelm had once seen him lift a hundred pound bag of oats over his head as though it weighed nothing. William was quiet and serious. He lived to work on the ranch. It was all he ever wanted and all he would ever need. He was struck down less than a week after Joe had died. His big muscles had done nothing to save him.

Leonore had been the next. She was the youngest, the family baby at twelve. Leonore had her father's round cheeks and an easy laugh which would ring across the yard. Her talk was always filled with jokes, and everything seemed funny to her. Leonore had been Wilhelm's favorite. She had been the joy of his life, the one thing that could make him smile when he was at his most dour. She was beautiful. She loved the world that she lived in more fully than anyone else Wilhelm had ever known.

Her laughter had turned to coughs, and she died just two weeks after her brother.

Felix had been the last. The middle child at fifteen. Felix never liked the ranch like his brother and sister did. He much preferred reading books to physical labor. He had been saving money so he could go to college. He wanted to become an accountant or a lawyer. He wanted to do the kind of work where he would never have to get his hands dirty again. Felix was always washing his hands. He hated the feel of dirt and grime on them. Felix's death had been a surprise. His brother and sister had died in November and after several months it seemed that the worst was over. Felix got sick and died in March. The same horrible symptoms had appeared, and all his parents' prayers went unanswered.

Wilhelm and Lilith had both gotten sick as well. They had both fallen ill soon after William's first symptoms had appeared. But where their children had steadily gotten worse and died, they got better. Their health returned, but their suffering continued. It made no sense. What kind of disease struck down the young and healthy, but spared the old? What kind of cruel god would play such a jest? Letting a man rise so far above his furthest dreams, and then snatch it all away in an instant?

Wilhelm sat at the graves for most of the afternoon. Not long ago, when he sat in the same place tears would run down his face in great rivulets and he would bawl like a small child. Now when he tried to cry nothing came out. His eyes remained dry and his face remained neutral. Wilhelm reached forward and touched each grave in turn. His voice was husky and barely audible. "Nicht lange," he said as he touched each cold stone. The declaration stirred nothing within him. He felt as though it should, but he just felt empty.

Wilhelm got up and walked back into the yard as the sun began to dip towards the horizon. He looked at all that he had made and felt nothing. What did it really matter now? None of it held any worth or value anymore. He walked back to the house and sat down at his fine well built wooden desk. It had been a gift from Lilith for his fortieth birthday. She had ordered it all the way from Kansas City. He opened a drawer that fit tightly into the frame and pulled out his ledger. Wilhelm flipped through the pages, the history of his success. The records all in German. He took out a fountain pen and made an entry just below the last one:

18 August 1920, Landwirtschaftliche Vorräte, Daniel Gibbs, $31.24

Wilhelm looked at the entry and wondered why he made it. He flipped through the book again. Past all the entries and clear through the still blank pages to the end. It was a strange feeling. Wilhelm felt like he should feel something, but he felt nothing. He was gone and all that was left was an empty body. On the last page, Wilhelm scrawled a message, his handwriting so rough that he had trouble reading it. He looked down at his writing and, like the last ledger entry, wondered why he bothered. Wilhelm closed the ledger and placed it back into its drawer.

Wilhelm stood up and stretched, and then walked back outside. He picked up one of the large cans of kerosene and carried it to the outhouse behind the house. The outhouse was a solid structure, its walls made of stone with a wooden roof and wooden door. Wilhelm stepped inside and poured the kerosene across the boards of the bench and the floor. He tossed the empty can outside and walked back to the porch. Wilhelm repeated the process with the second and third cans.

Wilhelm carried the fourth can into the outhouse. He sat on the wooden seat, the seat he had polished smooth so it would be more comfortable for Lillith, and left the door open so he could watch the setting sun. Wilhelm lifted the can of kerosene up and dumped it over his head. The hole below him was filled to the brim with wood and dry grass. Wilhelm had been very busy yesterday. Wilhelm pulled a small metal container full of matches from his pocket. He opened it and pulled out a single match. Wilhelm sat and watched the small orange flame burn down the stick towards his hand. There would undoubtedly be an easier way, a gun or a rope. Just a motion and then nothing. But Wilhelm was tired of feeling nothing. He wanted to feel something again, anything.

Wilhelm's tired eyes watched the flame burn. The sun slowly sank behind the hills and the sky turned red and orange. In his mind images of Lilith and his children flashed past in rapid motion. His voice was quiet, so quiet that though his lips moved no sounds came out.

"Ich bin fertig."

Wilhelm's fingers opened and the match dropped.

# Dirty Dozen

Oops
Oh my god.  I'm sorry.  I will pay for some new drapes.

Leaving
A lady deserves a taxi ride.  She got change for the bus.

Roleplaying
He made a good firefighter, until the candles dropped to the
floor.

Solitaire
If you're not ashamed of masturbating, then you're not doing it
right.

Ex
I didn't mind when she yelled his name.  The mask was
different.

Alternatives
She should've mentioned she didn't like it, before he started loving it.

Love
The I love you was not a lie, just a shortened sentence.

Relationship
You'll never understand, and I can't be the one to tell you.

Suggestion
It was not that it was inappropriate, as much as just disturbing.

Experimentation
That morning he couldn't meet her eye, nor hide his happy grin.

Rules
Was it really cheating on his wife, when he was technically alone?

Hate
She hated him so much that she had to have him now.

# The Desolate Shore

The ocean beat with the regularity of a human heart, each rolling wave both destroying and building the desolate gray sand of the shore. The tide rose and fell like clockwork, periodically inundating a narrow world with both sea and air. Great sheets of water rose from the depth and crashed against the stony walls of sea stacks, covered by birds of the great houses who rule their kingdoms jealously, though few, if any, could ford their salty moats or scale their rocky heights in order to challenge them. The desolate shore was a world always in motion, a place always changing, a world of harsh beauty.

Every morning, Wally woke up in his hut alone and got out of bed to light a fire and make himself porridge for breakfast. The porridge was bland stuff, but was cheap and kept well. Not yet ready to face the larger world around him he would eat in his hut, sitting on his bed, facing away from the doorway from which blew in sand, ocean spray, and morning sunshine. The wall, though plain and earthy, would shift and morph into mighty battles and courageous deeds as he barely chewed each morsel. When he finished they vanished, back whence they had come.

With breakfast done Wally would get up, put on his gray much patched clothes, and venture out onto the shore. His hut sat above the tide line against ancient sun dried trees blown in by wild wintry storms, surrounded by imposing sand dunes and covered by bladed shore grasses, their edges like saws against one's skin. Wally never noticed the sand dunes or the saw grasses, they had become a normal part of his world and no longer required noticing, much like ignoring the nose on one's own face. The ocean though was a different matter, the ocean always commanded Wally's attention. As soon as he walked out the door, it was there. The thunderous cacophony of its liquid state stretching from horizon to horizon. Wally would stare at it, his heart filled with a deep longing and yearning, for the barest of moments forgotten hopes and dreams would bubble up from his soul, but only for a moment. A deep bracing breath of salt air, and he would start the day's work.

Wally spent his mornings combing the beach, searching for treasures blown in by the ever moving waters. Seashells, driftwood, and treasures made by man and lost at sea, carried to him by the winds of fortune. Everything held value, but some things were more valuable than others. Things with the greatest value went into the old red wagon that Wally dragged behind him with a length of old hemp rope, the rear right wheel squeaking with every pull. The squeak was like that of a seagull and sometimes Wally would pretend he was one of the scavenging birds, flying above the beach, his sharp eyes combing the shore for bright baubles. The wagon moved easily across the smoothed sand, paved by the action of the waves, its wheels digging deeper furrows as its load increased.

As Wally worked, the real seagulls wheeled and dived around him, looking for the dead and the dying to fill their bellies, scavengers of a different type. Often Wally would ignore his feathered brethren, intent on his own work. However, sometimes, when pickings were few, he would sit and watch them flap and flutter. Wally would pretend that the seagulls could talk to him and he would have long and happy conversations, gossiping about the other birds, like the egret and the pelican, and talking of the wider world. The seagulls would tell him of distant lands that were unlike his own. Lands with colors that weren't washed out to gray by constant wind and rain. They would tell him of heroic kings and mighty deeds which they had seen.

If anyone could have seen Wally talking with the seagulls they would have surely thought he was insane, but this was never a worry. There were no people but him on the desolate shore. The closest people were the men of the village some way away, and their fishermen never came into the area, preferring the richer fishing grounds farther out to sea. Aside from the seagulls, no one but him ever walked the gray sands.

Lunch was always and invariably old dry crackers, or whatever porridge he had heated for breakfast but failed to eat. The afternoon was spent on more personal matters. Wally scoured the rocks and tide pools, looking for delicious underwater treats for a sea creature stew, or a clutch of unguarded eggs to be fried, poached, or boiled. The end of the day was spent on menial day to day tasks. Repairs to his hut, mending clothes and other belongings, gathering firewood, and carrying water from a nearby stream.

Every month Wally made the long fifteen mile journey to the village, dragging all that he had found in his wagon, or carrying it on his back in his old worn knapsack. The village sat on a round harbor guarded by jetty's which protected it from the wildness of the sea. Wally did not like the village, he found it crowded and its people crass, dirty, and rude. He would not stay long, just enough to sell his scavenged goods for a few copper pennies, and possibly peek into certain shops that met his interests. A tailor's shop where he could buy needle and thread, a market where he could buy porridge and crackers, and the tinsmith where he could buy the materials to repair his pots.

Across from the tinsmith was the cartographer's shop. Each time Wally went to the one, he would always find himself insatiably drawn to the window of the other. Through the window he would gaze at the brightly colored maps that showed the world far and away from the village and the desolate shore. A world of dreams and hopes. Wally's eyes would eagerly eat up every detail so that he could try to recreate their beauty in the sand outside of his hut. The cartographer, a man with the wonders of the world at his fingertips, would watch but make no move to try and garner a sale. Wally never actually entered the shop.

In the evening, Wally ate dinner, either the found eggs or sea creatures, or barring those, another helping of porridge. Wally did not mind the porridge, though he did not necessarily like it either. It was simply something to fill a hungry belly, something to keep him alive until the next day. Sometimes, if it were a special occasion, like a holiday or his birthday, he would purchase dried fruit at the village to mix in with his porridge. It was a rare treat, the exquisite taste of sweetness bringing a smile to his face.

After dinner was finished he would walk to a nearby rock, which jutted from the shore into the ocean in defiance of the howling wind and crashing waves. On this rock he would sit, looking out at the undulating cold waters and watching the sun slowly dip below the ocean, until even its magnificence was extinguished by the unending blue-gray plain. As it fell the sun would reach out with its golden arms, caressing the world which it loved one last time before it slipped beneath the waves. Wally would watch the sun die, and imagine himself upon the ocean, travelling to far and distant lands, seeing himself setting foot in the paradise that must surely await on the other side. His heart always grew heavy as he looked outwards, away from his desolate shore, but the sea was vast, and he was so small.

When the last rays of light dropped below the horizon he would return to his hut and go to sleep. Dreams of a better life would fill his head and each morning he would awake with a salty wetness on his cheeks.

One morning Wally could not venture forth as he normally did. A great storm was blowing across the ocean and the waves rose to never before seen heights. The winds howled and rain fell so hard that Wally could hardly tell where the sky ended and the sea began. Lightning lit the heavens as the gods of the above and the gods of the deeps battled for dominance over the world. For three days the battle raged, the waters rising right up to the doorstep of the hut. On the fourth day the seas receded, the rains stopped, the winds slowed, and all went back to how it had been before.

Wally woke on the morning of the fourth day and saw that the storm had passed. He lit his fire, ate his porridge, put on his clothes, and walked out to meet the new day. Wally gazed across the ocean, as he did every morning, his eyes scanned the horizon, resting on nothing, for all was already known. But wait, not all was known this morning. For there, standing upon the rock that jutted out into the ocean, in the same place he stood every evening, was a figure, looking out at the sea. Wally's breath sucked in with panic and he scurried back into the safety of his hut.

From the doorway he looked out at the mysterious figure. It was a person, tall and lithe, wrapped in homespun, black hair and a green shawl fluttering in the wind. What were they doing here? Wally had never seen anyone ever upon the desolate shore. Was it a villager? What were they doing here?

Wally watched the figure, who did nothing but stand and watch the ocean for the entire day. He did not know what to do or what to think. Nothing before in his life, remembered or imagined, had ever happened like this. He was captivated and perplexed, enthralled and horrified. Eventually the sun set on the far horizon over the sea and darkness fell upon the beach. Wally crawled back into bed, but did not sleep. His eyes watched the blanket that covered his hut's doorway.

The next morning Wally awoke and ate cold porridge since he had collected no wood the previous day for his fire. He looked out his doorway, his eyes ignoring all details but the rock jutting out into the ocean. The figure still stood there, looking out at the churning deeps. Wally stood for a moment, wracked by indecision, and then walked out of his hut, grabbed the rope to his wagon, and headed off down the beach away from the rock and the figure standing upon it. Mysterious figure or not, things still had to get done.

For three days Wally ignored the figure and continued on with his life, changing nothing in his routine except no longer sitting on the rock each evening to watch the sunset. Wally now spent his evenings sitting next to his hut, staring at the figure until darkness hid the beach from view. He was curious about the figure. Not even the seagulls with whom he talked seemed to know anything about it. He was scared of the figure. What kind of unnamed horror had come to roost at his desolate shore? Why was it here? What did it want?

On the fourth day Wally's curiosity became too much. As he scavenged along the shore he kept his head down and slowly worked his way toward the jutting rock. Step by step, combing the sand for treasures, but not really interested in finding any. Slowly but surely getting closer to the figure, taking a circuitous route to try and make it appear he had no interest in getting any closer. Three steps towards, one step back, a dance with no discernible order but an ever closing end. Shift through the sand, pick up a nice shell, four steps toward, one step back. Finally he stood crouched where sand, ocean, and rock all met. Warily he lifted his eyes from the gray granules, and looked at the figure standing above him.

It was a woman. She stood tall as a man. She was a large woman, not fat, just imposing, an Amazon blotting out the sky. A damp homespun dress clung to her curves, its fringes flapping in the gentle wind. Her bare arms crossed gently beneath her breasts, her body gently swaying with the breeze. A green shawl wrapped around her head, holding down long dark hair that framed her pale face. All of this Wally noted in an instant. Even a hermit such as himself could see how beautiful she was, but it was her eyes that held him captivated. Her eyes were the color of the ocean, as though they were only mirrors, reflecting back out into the world all that she surveyed. They seemed to leap from her face like two great beams of light, seeing everything, whether it be revealed or hidden.

Wally stared at her in silence for some time. Finally, feeling awkward, he opened his mouth to speak. No sound came, his tongue had become heavy. He closed his mouth, licked his lips and tried again.

"Hello."

It sounded far away. The woman started and looked down at him. Wally felt the full power of her eyes come upon him. He saw sadness, longing, storms long blown out, and gathering clouds of new storms in the future. He looked into her gaze and found himself stammering.

"M..m..my name is Wally."

The woman continued to stare and Wally felt her gaze burrow into his, deep into his mind, into the hidden recesses of his internal world. He felt naked, bare for all the world to see, but he would not, could not look away. The woman tilted her head to the side and smiled. Wally felt a wave of contentment cross over him.

"What's your name?"

The woman did not answer, she only looked at him, still smiling, the storm in her eyes turning into a calm sea. She broke the mutual gaze, and looked back out towards the ocean. Wally felt himself reemerge as though he was swimming from a great depth. He looked up at the woman, waiting for an answer. When he realized he would not get one he turned and walked back to his hut, dragging his wagon as he went.

That night he made a stew of crabs and kelp. As he sat by his hut preparing to eat he looked up at the figure standing on the rock. Shaking his head he took his bowl and carried it down the beach. Shyly he approached the rock, not daring to look up again and face the woman's watery eyes. He reached upwards and deposited the bowl near her feet.

"It's tidepool stew."

The woman said nothing, did not even look down to acknowledge his existence.

"It's good."

Seeing no reaction he turned and walked back to his hut to prepare for the next day.

The next morning the bowl was empty. Wally walked down to the rock first thing when he awoke. The woman was still staring out at the rolling waves.

"I told you it was good."

She did not answer. Wally smiled as he carried the bowl back to his hut. He cleaned it with care in the stream and then made his porridge. He made more than he normally did. Wally put the extra in the freshly cleaned bowl and added a little dried fruit that he had purchased the last time he was in the village and had been saving for his birthday. Cradling the bowl in his hands he carried it back and without a word deposited it on the rock next to the woman.

In silence he walked back to his hut. As he neared the doorway he felt her eyes upon him as they had been the day before. He turned and saw her observing him as he walked.

Wally prepared and ate his own breakfast, watching the woman from the corner of his eye. She stared at him for a bit, then kneeled down, lifted the bowl, and began to eat. Wally raised his hand in a wave. Hesitantly, the woman raised her own arm and returned the gesture, awkwardly as though she had never done it before.

Wally finished his breakfast and walked over to the stream, washed the pot in the stream, rubbing it clean with sand, and then carried it back into his hut. When he reemerged the woman was gone. At first Wally thought she had been sucked upward into the sky, disappearing as quickly as she had appeared. But then he saw her walking across the beach to the stream. The woman kneeled and scrubbed the bowl clean with sand, just as Wally had done with the pot. She then walked towards him. Wally felt his heart skip a beat and his breath became ragged. She walked right up to him, smiled, and put the bowl into his hands. Wally took it dumbly, and watched her walk back to her rock, each step leaving a small footprint in the sand. Wally gazed after her until she took her place, and then returned the bowl to its place on the shelf above his bed.

Wally worked that day, never venturing too far from the rock or his hut. As he worked, stooped over, digging through the sand, he felt the woman watching him. She watched as he scooped up shells and put them in his wagon. She watched as he searched the tide pools and rocky bird nests for tasty morsels. Every movement, every action, was gazed upon with a keen interest. Wally felt himself become clumsy, fumbling and making mistakes in ways he had never done. He had never had someone watch him work before, or even show any interest in doing so.

That evening, Wally made a mixture of porridge and pelican eggs. He filled the bowl and carried it and the pot to the rock. He placed the bowl next to the woman and then sat in the sand not far away and began to eat. The woman picked up the bowl and stood looking from it to him. Finally she climbed down from the rock, walked over, and sat cross legged nearby. They ate in silence, both staring out at the endless depths. When she finished, the woman turned towards him and smiled. Her mouth moved, contorting into weird shapes it was obviously not used to making.

"Th...than...thank you."

In Wally's mind, old automatic responses, long left unused, sparked back to life.

"You're welcome."

The woman got up, climbed back onto her rock, and sat, looking out at the sea. Wally watched until she was settled, then picked up the bowls, and walked back to his hut.

So it was for some time that things continued as they were. Wally would do his daily work as he had always done, and the woman with the ocean in her eyes would watch from her rock. Things were not the same as they had been. When Wally found an interesting shell, or some valuable treasure from some far off shipwreck, he would rush back to the rock to show her, eager as a child. She would always smile at the treasures that he brought. For the first time since he had come to the desolate shore, Wally felt a feeling of satisfaction in his work, pride for his skills, pleasure in what he did.

Each morning, noon, and evening he would make enough food for two, and eat with her, sitting in the sand next to the rock. Together they would stare out at the sea. She would say nothing. Sometimes Wally would talk at great lengths, of the things he had found or seen that day, or of an interesting tidbit told to him by the seagulls. Other times he would sit with her in silence, watching the waves crash against the shore. It was in these times, these silent times, that he felt a great wave of contentment like he had never known wash over him. He would go to sleep at night in his hut with a smile, and wake with his face dry.

Wally did not venture beyond the sight of the woman. Part of him worried that if he ventured too far, the woman would not be there when he got back. He did not want the woman to be gone. He did not want her to disappear as quickly as she had arrived. She was by far the nicest treasure he had ever found on the beach. For the first time in his life he feared loneliness. No matter what he wanted though, something had to be done. Pickings within sight of the rock were becoming fewer and fewer. He could not continue to comb the same section of beach again and again.

That night as he ate with the woman next to the rock he told her what he had to do. He explained that he would have to venture further afield. He explained that the sand around the rock had been picked clean. That it would take time for the ocean to bring more treasures to that part of the shore. The woman listened in silence, a look of concentration and confusion on her sad face. Wally did not know if she understood, but the next day, he swallowed his worries and began walking farther down the beach. As the rock receded behind him he turned and waved. The woman excitedly waved back and he smiled. He walked further, feeling his sadness and worry grow with each step. He turned to wave again, but the rock was empty.

The woman was jogging across the sand towards him, running to catch up. Wally started in surprise, and then he smiled. He had never seen the woman so far from her rock before. He had never seen any kind of inclination that maybe he was as important to her as she was to him. Wally's smile grew larger and larger as she got closer. When she arrived next to him she looked quizzically at his toothy grin, and then smiled back. Wally felt a great wave of happiness wash over him, drowning him in joy and contentment.

Together they walked down the gray shore. At first the woman stayed close to him and the wagon, never venturing more than a few feet away. However, as they walked, her head constantly swung back and forth, drinking in all of the sights and sounds. The day was bright, sunny, and warm. All of the things that had long since become unnoticed by Wally seemed to fill her with wonder. The seagulls circling and calling to each other in the air, diving down only long enough to fight over a dead fish or other morsel. Crabs scuttling quickly across the sand, looking for new tide pools to hide in until the ocean rose and reclaimed its lost fragments. Saw-grass along the dunes swaying softly in the coastal breeze. The ocean rolling playfully onto the beach, advancing and retreating.

The woman's head suddenly quit moving. Her eyes stared across the sand. Wally turned to see what she was looking at, and caught a glimpse of a bit of white sticking out of the sand at the edge of the high water mark. The woman leaped forward, blocking his view. Long white legs propelled her forward. She reached down where her eyes were staring and scooped the white thing out of the mass of silica. She ran back across the sand, cupping the white object in her hands. Her mouth smiling and her eyes dancing she held out her treasure to him. It was a whole sand dollar. Wally took it carefully from her hands, and wiped the loose sand from its surface. She looked at him eagerly. He looked up at her and smiled, then carefully placed it in the wagon. The woman laughed and clapped her hands, and ran down the beach to find more.

After that the woman was his constant companion as he scoured the beach. While he trudged through his daily routine she would run and dance across the gray sand, whooping in delight at each new discovery. Wally was amazed by her energy. She never seemed to slow down, never seemed to tire. She would point and laugh at the antics of the birds. Once she pulled him to a tide pool so she could show him how the sea anemones closed when she touched them with her finger. Another time she pointed out to sea and cooed with delight at the sight of distant whales throwing up great streams of water from their blowholes. Wally delighted in seeing her so excited. She was better at finding treasures then he was. Nothing escaped her gaze. She would often come running back across sand that he thought empty, carrying something that he had missed.

She would follow him almost anywhere. A few times he tried to coax her into his hut, but she shied away from its darkness. She would sit outside and watch him cook on his little stove. Once her curiosity overcame her fear, and she ventured inside. She quickly left in a panic and raced across the sand back to the rock where he had first found her. She did not venture from it again until the next evening. When it came time to go to town she at first followed him, but when they came within sight of the distant buildings she froze and quickly moved away. Wally tried to wave her forward, but she turned and ran back up the shore. When he returned from the village, he found her sitting on her rock, shivering and waiting for him. Wally was worried, but the dried fruit he had brought back for her quickly set her to rights.

They sat on the beach later than normal that night. They both ate their meals in silence and then he talked and told her of the wonders he had seen in town. Of the strange people at the market, the kind old tinsmith in his dark musty shop, and of the bright maps in the cartographer's window. They sat in silence and contentment as the green flash heralded the final setting of the sun. One by one the stars began to fill the sky, ancient far off gods, some long dead before their light reached across the heavens to the sight of Wally and the woman with the ocean in her eyes. Wally sat, enraptured, feeling small before the immensity all around him.

Her hand rested next to his. He leaned in close and told the stories of the different constellations. Stories told to him long ago by his long gone mother. Filling in the parts from imagination that he could no longer remember. Horrid monsters, mighty heroes, jilted lovers, pain, sacrifice, selfishness, and selflessness. All of the best and worst of humanity wheeled above them. A shooting star streaked across the sky and Wally felt his hand move over, his fingers brush the top of hers. The woman jerked back in surprise. She turned her head and looked at him, her head tilted to the side, her eyes staring into him quizzically. Wally felt his face flush with embarrassment. He smiled weakly and then looked back quickly at the stars. He could feel the woman's eyes boring into the side of his head. The woman wrapped her arm around him and laid her head on his shoulder. Wally stiffened, not use to such contact with another. The woman sighed happily. The heavens continued their slow march overhead.

The next day they awoke in each other's arms upon the sand. Wally woke first. He walked back up to his hut and made breakfast for the two of them. By the time he returned she was awake also, brushing the sand out of her hair with her fingers. They ate in silence as they always did. After they were done eating, Wally dug a hole in the sand and the woman watched with patient expectation and curiosity. Only a foot down the sand became very wet. He scooped up a handful and squeezed it in front of him. Drip by drip, piece by piece, a tiny tower formed on the sand below. Sections grew and sometimes toppled, but all added to the organic curves of his creation.

Wally hadn't made drip castles since he was very young. They were part of a distant memory, a recollection of times when life was more than just work and hardship. A time when everything was new, and every day brought with it new hopes and dreams. It had been a long time. Flashes of his mother swept across Wally's mind. It had been a long time since Wally had cared for anyone. It had been a long time since Wally had felt cared for.

The woman delighted in the drip castles and quickly reached into the hole and began constructing her own. Wally watched as she smiled and laughed, her tower growing and collapsing again and again. Each collapse added to the foundation, and each tower climbed slightly higher than the last. She was beautiful, the most beautiful thing he had ever seen. She could feel him watching her. She looked up and smiled at him, before returning to the creation of her own private kingdom.

The sand was gray, the sky was gray, the rocks were gray, the saw grass was gray, the driftwood was gray. Everything was gray. The shore was desolate. Wally fit into his surroundings, he was a part of them, he was as gray as the rest. The woman did not belong here. She was a shining star in an empty sky. She radiated her light around her, drawing the eye in. Wally had never noticed the desolation around him before. He had never noticed how ugly the world was that he lived in. He could see it now. Wally felt guilty. Wally felt bad. The desolate shore was not the place for this woman. She did not belong there. She belonged in a better place. Wally took the woman's sandy hands in his own.

"Where did you come from?"

The woman only looked back at him in silence, and for a moment her eyes became shaded and covered. The light from them dimmed.

"What brought you here to me? How was it that I found you sitting on that rock outside my hut?"

The woman stared at him, a worried look upon her face.

"I never imagined anything like you. I want to give you everything that your heart desires. What is the thing that you want the most?"

The woman smiled and gave his hands a squeeze. Wally smiled back.

"I'll give you anything."

The woman's smile faded and she gave his hands another squeeze before letting go. She got up and climbed back onto her rock. Her eyes gazed out across the ocean. Wally watched her stare out into the depths. He could feel the yearning in her. The yearning for something he could not provide. The yearning for the open sea.

It took some time to make the preparations. Wally dug up a wooden box buried in the sand behind his hut and took it into the village the next morning. He went down to the wharf and there amongst the fishermen traded the majority of what was in the box for a small boat. The boat was only twelve feet long, and well weathered from many days at sea. A short squat cabin sat in its front for shelter from the elements. A single mast jutted from the deck upward into the sky. With the remainder of the contents of the box he bought supplies. Fishing gear, water casks, extra rope, hammer and nails for repairs, porridge, and dried fruit. He sailed the boat from the village, it had been a long time, but he still remembered how to sail, and beached it near his home.

The woman watched him in silence from her rock as he walked back and forth between the beached boat and his hut, carrying his meager belongings. His body shook as he did so. The sea. The sea had always filled him with awe at its beauty and wonder. The sea had always beckoned him, pulled at him, promised a better world. Wally was afraid of the sea. On the sea one could be free, one could sail anywhere they wanted, the possibilities were endless. The sea was big and the sea was wide. The sea was huge and he was small. The sea could destroy him and all that he was in the blink of an eye. The sea did not love, the sea did not care. It was a risk to sail on the sea, a risk to leave the desolate shore behind. There were no guarantees. The desolate shore was bare and empty, but it was known, and it was safe.

Back and forth he trudged between hut and boat. Bowls, blankets, utensils. All of his possessions. They had never seemed so meager before, never seemed so small. The hut was empty after only two trips. The woman climbed down from the rock and walked over to stand beside him. Together they looked out at the breakers. She looked at him and pointed out at the horizon. Wally looked back and nodded. The woman smiled and reached forward, grabbing his hands. Wally could not tell if the shaking he felt came from him or her.

The next morning they pushed the boat out into the water until the waves lifted it to float above the bottom. Wally ran up the sail and the wind caught it, pushing the tiny construct of wood, paint, and canvas forward. As the boat began to move away from the shore the woman stood in the front, smiling, water spraying up over her, glistening like diamonds on her skin. Wally, at the tiller, looked back at the rock and the gray shore. He looked back at his squat hut, its empty black door, and the beat up old red wagon sitting in front of it. His hands tightened around the tiller until his knuckles turned white, but he forced himself to look forward until the coast disappeared behind them beneath the horizon.

The open sea was a scary place. The ocean was never still and the boat constantly moved upward and downward, climbing and falling from one wave to the next. There was no land in sight. Wally could stand up in the boat, search every horizon, and see nothing. It was frightening to see nothing. It was frightening to know that your life depended on a few pieces of shaped wood primitively held together. At first the seagulls were a constant companion. Visitors from the far off shore. Wally thought of them as old friends. But as the shore grew farther away their visits became less regular, until even they were gone. They were truly alone, him and the woman with the ocean in her eyes.

Wally was scared of the ocean, but he was happy to be sailing upon it. Each day they would take turns directing the boat as it was blown forward by the wind towards a distant constellation. Neither were good sailors, but they swiftly learned, quickly figuring out what had to be done to direct their little craft. Each day they would fish in hopes of catching their dinner. Wally took great pleasure in the fishing, in the careful casting, in the patient waiting, in the pitched battle when a fish was foolish enough to take the bait. If they failed to catch a fish they would eat from their stores. At first Wally would leave the guts out for the birds. When they quit coming he just threw them over the side instead.

At night they laid together in the blankets under the roof of the small cabin, their heads sticking out into the open so they could see the stars. They would stare up at the constellations, caressing each other. The woman would slowly fall asleep in the crook of Wally's arm. As her breathing slowed and she dropped off into the world of dreams, Wally would feel completely and utterly at peace. The desolate shore that he had called his home for so long seemed so far away. A distant memory. Wally would have called his previous life a dream if he didn't feel like he was dreaming now. Sometimes he worried that he was dreaming and that he would awaken to find himself in his hut again. Alone.

The woman delighted in swimming. When the waves were calm and the sails slack she would dive into the water and swim about the boat in great circles. Her body seemed to turn to liquid as she swam, as though she was becoming one with the world around her. She would laugh and motion for Wally to join her, but he refused. The thought of swimming in the ocean petrified him. He was not a strong swimmer. If he left the boat it would surely float away beyond his measly skills to return to it. The ocean was full of monsters. The ocean was a monster. It could destroy him so easily. He loved to watch her swim, but when he did his body would begin to shake and his hands tighten. The woman would laugh and beckon again. He would smile back weakly and wave. She would smile and see how deeply she could dive.

When she returned to the boat all of his fears would be forgotten. Once a pod of dolphins swam by and entertained them with their antics. They leapt high out of the water and did flips. The woman laughed and clapped her hands. Some swam right next to the boat and stuck their heads out of the water. They talked in their squeaky dolphin language and let the woman pat their heads as though they were trained dogs looking for a treat. She pulled Wally forward and made him pet them as well. Their skin was wet and rubbery. As soon as he touched them they let loose a squeaky laugh and swam away. The woman beamed at him and he felt proud.

The ocean is a fickle world. The calm seas do not remain calm forever. One morning the waves rose higher than they normally did. The boat climbed up steep hills, raced to the bottom, and then started climbing once again. The skies darkened with great black clouds marching across the sky, obliterating the blue and the sunlight. The air crackled with energy and the winds picked up and began to howl. Wally quickly took down the canvas of the sail. He had lived his whole life next to the ocean. He knew its power and its fury, but he had never seen it unchained, no solid land to hold down the beast. The woman's face was filled with fear and she shivered in her fright. She went into the small cabin, and hid her head beneath the blankets.

The rain began to fall, the first few random drips turning into a torrential wall of water. The clouds emitted evil laughs of thunder and lightning skipped across the heavens. The waves grew high and crashed downwards with deafening force. The winds howled like a pack of banshees on the hunt for souls. The storm rolled across the sea and the tiny boat was but a cork in a splashing giant's bathtub. Wally fought the storm, he fought it with all his might. Wally braved the winds and rain. Desperately trying to hold the boat on a steady course he lashed himself to the tiller. Grimly trying to keep the boat from being rolled into the briny depths, he screamed obscenities at the sky, but the storm only laughed back and unleashed more of its evil power. A great crack from above and the top third of the mast ripped away, twisting through the sky like a leaf in the wind, and then nothing.

Wally awoke to find himself still tied to the tiller. The boat floated upon a wobbling sea, the sky a dull blue, the sun shining through the remains of the storm as it continued on its way, a black wall on the horizon. Wally untied himself and crawled to the front of the boat. There he found the woman, lying against the side, hiding from the sun, her eyes filled with fear and fixed in front of her. She was shaking. Wally took her in his arms and held her tight. They had made it. They had survived.

"Everything's all right," he cooed, "everything is all right."

The woman did not turn her gaze, it was the only part of her that did not waver.

"The boat is sinking."

"What?"

Wally looked about him in confusion. The boat was damaged, there was no doubt about that, but it certainly was not sinking.

"No we're not. We're just fine. It was just a little storm."

The woman stared at the side of the boat opposite from where she sat.

"The boat is sinking."

Wally looked at her, at her eyes filled by an unfathomable fear. They no longer glinted as they once had. He could no longer see the light in them, it was as though she had gone away. Wally looked where her distant eyes gazed. He leaned close and examined every board and every seam. The inside of the boat was bone dry. He looked back at the woman in confusion.

"The boat is going to sink."

Wally tried to hold her a little longer, but it did nothing. She just sat there and stared forward. He tried to comfort her and coax her to come up from the depths where she had retreated, but she just stared forward and repeated her mantra. Wally went into the cabin and got hammer, nails, and the extra wood they carried to plug leaks. He set to work hammering over every crack, crevice, and knothole. He looked at her and she said it again.

"The boat is sinking."

Desperation set in, he tore apart the little cabin, piece by piece, and used the scrap to cover leaks that did not exist. Board on top of board, a great heavy mass that turned their once graceful craft into an ungainly crate floating upon the open ocean. When the cabin was completely disassembled he began removing braces and pieces of the boat itself. Wally was overcome with madness, desperately trying to stop a leak that only the woman with the ocean in her eyes could see. The woman began to cry and let out a hysterical wail again and again.

"The boat is sinking, the boat is sinking, the boat is sinking."

Wally dropped his hammer and the few remaining nails and turned back to her. The boat listed heavily to one side and the nails rolled back towards the lump of wood weighing it down. He grabbed her arms and shook her gently.

"The boat is not going to sink. There is no leak. We're safe. It was just a little storm. It's going to be all right. We're not going to sink."

A single large wave, a sneaker wave the mariners call it, rose from the briny depths and struck the side of the boat. The once strong hull creaked and groaned and the weight of Wally's repairs pulled downward into the sea. For just a second everything hung in the balance, and then the boat flipped and

broke up, its once solid structure torn asunder. Wally
desperately clung to the remains of the mass. He saw the woman
holding onto the tiller not far away. He kicked towards her,
calling for her. For a moment their eyes met, and for a moment
it was her again, her eyes filled with joy and hope. Wally
reached out his hand to her and she raised her hand to meet his.

It was only for a moment. The woman broke his gaze and
looked behind him at the retreating storm. Her shoulders sagged
and her hand fell back into the water. The fear returned to her
eyes and she retreated back into herself. She turned her head
away, salt water running down her cheeks. Wally cried out for
her again, but she did not seem to hear. She let go of the tiller.
She began to kick her legs, propelling herself away from Wally,
who sat and watched in dumb puzzlement. He began to kick his
legs as hard and fast as he could, desperate to catch her,
desperate to stop her. The woman kicked harder. The woman
kicked faster. The woman could swim better than he could.
Wally was weighed down by the weight of the mast.

Slowly the distance between them became greater. Wally
called out to the woman again. He let go of the mast, to alleviate
himself of its anchoring weight, but quickly grabbed it again as
he felt the ocean begin to suck him down. Wally kicked harder
but now the currents had him and he watched in silent
desperation as the figure of the woman grew more distant, soon
only visible at the crest of each bobbing wave, and then gone.

Tears filled Wally's eyes. Screams of anguish and grief
filled his lungs. He thought of letting go of the mast and
swimming after her, but he knew he would never catch her
before he drowned. His spirit and body were exhausted, he
could no longer fight the world around him. He fell into a
stupor, and let the world do with him what it would.

Wally woke sometime later on his belly, his face half buried
in gritty sand, gentle waves rolling upward to cover him like a
chilly blanket, before retreating to let the cheerful sun warm his

soaked and weary body. Flotsam and jetsam rode the waves around him, pushed further ashore with each movement. Wally raised himself on his arms and breathed deeply. He stood and looked about him, slowly gazing at the strange desolate beach around him. He turned and looked at the rolling surface of the ocean that had spat him upon the mysterious shore. He stared out at its mighty depths and tears rolled down his cheeks.

# Previously Published Works

**One Night In Rapid City**
First published in *Bull*, October 2018

**The Heartbreaker**
First published in *The Soundings Review*, Winter 2015

**Digory**
First published in *The Punch Magazine*, Spring 2019

**Lugnut**
First published in *The MacGuffin*, Volume 32, Number 2, Winter 2016

**Poison**
First published in *Red Rock Review*, Issue 42, Spring 2018

# Dates Written

| | |
|---|---|
| One Night In Rapid City | June 2013 |
| The Heartbreaker | March 2013 |
| Chariots In The Sky | May 2013 |
| Knit Your Own Cat | April 2013 |
| The Golden Room | April 2013 |
| The Rusty Bike | March 2013 |
| Giggles | April 2013 |
| Digory | March 2013 |
| Gooning 101 | April 2013 |
| Nugget | October 2013 |
| Melancholy | April 2013 |
| An E-Mail | April 2013 |
| Lugnut | July 2013 |
| The Green Monster | April 2013 |
| The Cowboy | August 2013 |
| Molly | March 2013 |
| Rant Of A Snarky Scientist | November 2013 |
| Forgive Me Father For You Have Sinned | May 2013 |
| The Letter | April 2013 |
| Bear Rug | September 2013 |
| Grammie | March 2013 |
| Poison | April 2013 |
| Crazy, I Was Crazy Once | March 2013 |
| Ich Bin Fertig | November 2013 |
| Dirty Dozen | November 2013 |
| The Desolate Shore | March 2013 |

# Also Written By The Author

## *The Uncanny Valley*

We all know a Paul. A person who seems to see stuff that isn't there. The type the polite call quirky and the blunt call nuts. Conspiracies? He's got a few. He's got his finger on how the world really works. He knows what kind of shit is coming down the pipe. Flee across the West Texas desert to Mexico? Makes sense to him. Feel like you're being watched? You bet your ass someone is watching. Best turn off your cellphone. Troubles? Of course, that's just part of life. Doubts? No time for doubts. Shit is getting real. Get in, buckle up, crack open a beer. The only real question is, how far down the rabbit hole are you willing to follow?

## *An Unsated Thirst*

They say that an author's first stories are their most raw. Here is a collection of S.W. Campbell's first short stories and writings. Combining both published and unpublished works, An Unsated Thirst explores victory and defeat, triumph and shame, and an unflinching view of our naked selves. How one views such stories is dependent upon the mood of the reader. Whether we are at our highs or at our lows. However, it is hard for any of us to claim that such stories are ones that we cannot identify with. Contained within these pages are parts of our lives which we try to forget, though they are an important part of what makes us whole. Such stories should be embraced, accepted within ourselves so we can better accept them with others.

## *Papaya*

When a devastating hurricane hits the Caribbean island of Domenique, its inhabitants are forced into a singular struggle to survive and rebuild. Isolated in their midst is Ted, a Peace Corps volunteer who fled the ashes of his former life only to find himself labeled an outsider. Infatuated by the enigmatic wife of his only friend, Ted thrusts himself into a world beyond his comprehension. As obsession turns to desperation, tensions grow and Ted is forced to decide exactly how far he will go to rebuild amidst the muddy ruins.

## *Stumptown*

There are places where people say things are better. Where the downtowns do not empty after dark and people dare to dream beyond their means. Quirky utopias where the sins of the past are washed away by gentle rains and we all go forward arm in arm together into the brightening sunshine. Distant locations flocked to by young pilgrims, unencumbered by the deeply driven roots of age, where everything will be different. Combining both published and unpublished work, Stumptown is a collection of stories about ordinary people, navigating their personal anxieties and drama in a time when uncertainties were still tucked away and not allowed to distort the sense of hope in the air. It is a soliloquy to naivete, and the belief that a better world is a place rather than an idea.

## *The People's Republic of 47th & Long*

Perhaps the world would be a better place if we thought of ourselves less as good people, and more as lousy people who manage to do good things. My friend Leopold was always a dreamer. The pandemic and our reactions to it left us broken and divided. Most of us just wanted to feel safe again, but others dreamt of something better. Leopold was one of these. Though I think he likely joined the People's Republic of 47th and Long purely out of geographic convenience, I know once part of it, he fully shared in its egalitarian vision. All I have are his letters. Sometimes I wish I had burned them, but I didn't, so now here they are. Maybe you can find a use for them. Perhaps they can help remind you who we truly are. The good, the bad, and most importantly, the indifferent.

More information can be found at:

www.shawnwcampbell.com

# About The Author

S.W. Campbell was born in Eastern Oregon in 1983 after a harrowing drive through a fog. He currently resides in Portland, Oregon where he works as an economist and lives with a lovely house plant named Morton. He has had many short stories published in various literary reviews, some of which appear in this work, and has also self-published several books. His work can be found at www.shawnwcampbell.com.

www.ingramcontent.com/pod-product-compliance
Lightning Source LLC
Chambersburg PA
CBHW060629260626
47161CB00008B/2840